I live on a farm in the West of Ireland, with my husband and two children. We're farmers. We raise horses and cattle as a livelihood, not as a hobby or a pastime. The work is often hard and the hours long, especially in the summer months. Our children learn at an early age that they must help as well.

Piggy was an unexpected addition to our farm last year. He turned one ordinary summer into a whirlwind of events and emotions. We all grew to love him, especially my daughter who rode him.

This is a true story about Piggy, alias Timber Twig. I hope you'll enjoy reading it and share in all the ups and downs of that memorable summer.

Kate McMahon

Kate McMahon

Timber Twig

Illustrated by Terry Myler

THE CHILDREN'S PRESS

For
Oonagh Mary Hyland
for sharing Timber Twig with us

First published 1997 by
The Children's Press
an imprint of Anvil Books
45 Palmerston Road, Dublin 6

2 4 6 5 3

ISBN 1 901737 01 2

Typeset by Computertype Limited
Printed by Colour Books Limited

Contents

1	A Bad Start	7
2	Maggie	14
3	Off to the Show	20
4	Athenry	27
5	Disaster!	34
6	Nick	43
7	Country Blues	48
8	The Volunteer	57
9	Good News – Bad News	64
10	Loughrea	73
11	Three Letters	80
12	Heartbreak	87
13	Scariff	95
14	Dr Joyce	103
15	Mom Takes Charge	109
16	Two Miracles	117
17	Ballinasloe	125
18	The Parting of the Ways	136
	Glossary	140
	Author	142

1 A Bad Start

'Easy, Piggy, easy,' I coaxed. 'Talk to your pony,' Mom was always saying. 'It will pay in the long run.'

'What about the short run?' I thought. 'The here and now? Athenry next week?'

I tried to steady him as we headed towards the centre of the sand-ring. I sat deep into the saddle, and kicked him hard, asking him to pick up a canter. He did so willingly.

'Good boy, Piggy!' I praised before looking down at his canter lead. Then my heart sank when I saw that he had picked up the wrong lead again.

If you're not into horses (I am, as you've probably gathered) you won't know what on earth I'm talking about. Let me explain: the words 'canter lead' are used to describe the pony's leading leg. When he is cantering to the left, the left front leg should lead; when he is cantering to the right the right front leg should be leading. Vital in a figure-of-eight, an exercise used in ridden-class competitions.

'Piggy, what *is* wrong with you?' I wailed as I slowed him to a trot. This was the fourth time today that he had picked up the wrong canter lead and ruined the exercise. Piggy (real name Timber Twig, only nobody ever called him that except at shows) was playing up. Fourteen years old and very well schooled, he had been given to me on loan to ride and to take to the summer shows. But ever since we started to do ring work earlier in the week he'd been acting the right eejit.

But I wasn't going to give up easily. 'Come on, Pig, let's try it again,' I said in my most soothing voice. 'Rome wasn't built in a day.'

That was one of Dad's favourite sayings. I had, not one, but two parents who were always feeding me words of wisdom.

As I turned Piggy, my eye swept past the old familiar landmarks that surrounded our riding-ring – the blackthorn hedges thick with blossom, the massive chestnut-tree where Dad had rigged up a swing for my brother Sam and me, and the half-hidden roof of the old farmhouse that was home.

Then I saw something unfamiliar, something metallic, in a gap in the hedge. Two bicycles were drawn up against the fence.

'Hi, Clare! Having trouble with your new pony?' a voice called mockingly.

I recognised her. Kelly Lynch. Her father owned a seafood restaurant in Galway and the family had just built a mansion-style house next to our farm. She was the same age as me, but a class behind at school.

'Hi, Piggy!' called the second girl. I recognised her too: Brenda Fahy. One of the numerous hangers-on Kelly Lynch seemed to attract. Always around, hoping for a lift in the Merc, or to be asked to stay for supper, or invited into the judges' tent at the shows. Mr and Mrs Lynch were on every sponsor's list.

'Piggy by name and Piggy by nature,' Kelly added sarcastically.

They both sniggered. I turned away from them and began the figure-of-eight exercise again. Their voices reached me across the grass and sand.

'Kelly, isn't Athenry Show on this week-end?' This from Brenda.

'Tut, tut, tut! The judge won't like *that* figure-of-eight,' taunted Kelly.

'Are cart ponies allowed at the show?' inquired Brenda.

'I don't think so, unless there's a special class for farm animals,' snickered Kelly. 'She'd better stick to the lead-rein class.'

'And just look at those baggy jodhpurs. Out of the ark,' was the parting comment as they got on their bicycles and cycled away. I could hear their laughter from down the road. I hoped they both got punctures. Not that Kelly would – hers was a state-of-the-art mountain bike in whatever colours were due in next season.

I had pretended not to notice them, not to see them, not to hear their sneers. But now that I was alone, tears filled my eyes. Hot angry tears. I could feel my face burning with humiliation. I could just see Kelly parading around the showgrounds. New Barbour jacket. jodhpurs from Callaghans of Dublin. And, of course, imported leather jodhpur boots.

I couldn't ride any more. I dismounted Piggy and put up my stirrups. I led him back into the stable and into his roomy stall.

'Just my luck to blow it in front of them.' My anger began to grow as I untacked Piggy and hung up his saddle and bridle. 'I hope Kelly Lynch steps in cow-dung, and it fills her lousy shoes,' I cursed under my breath.

Piggy nuzzled me as I checked to see if his water bucket needed refilling.

'Oh, Piggy,' I whispered, 'why did you do this to me? Why won't you pick up the proper leads? Then Kelly and Brenda would have nothing to sneer about. Why did you let me down?'

Piggy's dark-brown eyes looked at me. His nose continued to nuzzle me in search of the apple I always brought him after our ride. I clasped my arms around his neck and hugged him close for a moment. It wasn't his fault, but I wouldn't give him his apple just yet.

Latching his stable door, I ran across the yard and in through the back door. There was a small utility room that led, if you turned one way, into the kitchen or, if you went straight on, up the back stairs.

I looked briefly into the kitchen. Mom and Dad were there. Mom was at the range taking out a tray of brown scones. I was surprised to see Dad sitting at the kitchen table, with his sheep-dog Rex stretched out at his feet. He wasn't usually home at this hour. He should still have been drawing in hay bales from the front meadow.

'Clare? Back already?' My mother's voice held a query. 'I thought you were going to have a good long training session on Piggy.'

'You thought wrong,' I shouted angrily, letting the back door slam. 'I'm never going to ride that pony again. And I'm never going to wear those hand-me-down jodhpurs again. You're making me look like a fool in front of my friends. And you can forget the shows. Get Sam. I'm finished with ponies.'

I had only time to take in their startled disbelieving looks as Mom dropped her oven-glove and Dad looked up from some letter he was reading.

Then I raced upstairs and slammed my bedroom door shut. I threw myself on my bed and burst into tears.

My tears lasted all of ten minutes. Then I began to feel slightly better. And slightly guilty. Was this really me? Slamming doors. Shouting. All because of a bold pony and a couple of stuck-up girls. I felt sorry for Dad. He didn't approve of tantrums – especially mine. Mom and I understood one another, even to slamming doors. 'God never shuts one door but he opens another,' was another of her favourite sayings. There was a tacit acceptance that He knew all about shutting, if not slamming, doors.

I decided to wait a while before I went back downstairs. I lay back on my bed and propped my head up with two pillows. I wondered what Mom was making for tea. Sausages and mash? Rashers and fried eggs? Or perhaps my favourite – rashers on toast, with crispy pan-fried potatoes.

My eyes scanned the bedroom walls which were plastered with horse posters and pony magazine cut-

outs. There were showjumpers, including Boome-
rang the pride of the Irish, and Milton the pride of
the English, and racehorses like Dawn Run, the
famous mare, winning the Champion Hurdle, and
Desert Orchid, the legendary grey who stole the
hearts of thousands. I had newspaper clippings of
Danoli, the racehorse from Carlow who broke his leg,
only to recover and win again. There were posters of
Red Rum and Arkle and Aldaniti, each with his own
story of fame and glory. And the stallion Shergar,
worth millions, kidnapped from his stable and never
seen again.

I thought long and hard about Kelly. She was the
girl who had everything. Looks, including long,
thick, blonde hair (mine was thin and mousy-brown,
even if it did have what Mom called 'nice highlights'
when the sun shone on it), clothes by the yard – she
never wore anything twice – and doting parents who
only seemed to exist to give her everything she
wanted.

That included an expensive pony that was going to
run rings around Piggy and me at Athenry this week-
end. We would be in the same class: Working Hunter
Pony 133, ridden by a child under the age of
fourteen. The 133 bit means that the pony must not
be any taller than 133 centimeters at his wither, the
point where the pony's neck and back meet (I'm not
making this up - it's all in the pony manual).

The class itself has two parts. In the first, each
rider has to jump a course of at least eight fences.
The judge awards up to ten points for how each

fence is jumped and there are additional points for the way rider and pony tackle the course. There are penalties for refusals and knock-downs. Usually the six with the best scores are invited back for part two. Each has to do an individual test – walking, trotting, and the dreaded figure-of-eight, ending up with a gallop around the ring.

Then it's all over, bar the shouting. The three riders with the best overall scores receive rosettes – red for first, blue for second, yellow for third. Finally, everyone gallops around the ring to the cheers of parents, families and friends, the winners with rosettes in hand. Great for the top three, pretty awful for the tail-enders; even worse for those who don't make the final six.

As to the winner, I guessed it would be Kelly. I felt I didn't have a chance. What judge would be able to resist the combination of such a beautifully turned-out girl and a flashy thoroughbred pony called Moonstepper. Especially one who got her figure-of-eight right. I knew she would, after all the private lessons I heard she'd been having.

Maybe if I asked Mom and Dad nicely they might give me an early Christmas gift of a decent pair of jodhpurs. Then at least I'd feel I looked all right.

I sighed deeply, reached over and picked up a well-worn copy of *Horse and Pony*. The magazine had a special article on training a pony to do the perfect figure-of-eight.

2 Maggie

I must have dozed off because I suddenly awoke with a start. Someone was throwing small stones against the window. I got up and looked out. It was Maggie, my best friend in all the world.

'What are ye doin' in bed? It's only six. Are ye sick or something?' she called.

'No,' I replied, sounding sad.

'Yer mam said ye're pussin' about something. Can I come up? She said I can stay for tea. It'll be ready in a bit.'

'Come on up. I'll fill you in on the latest,' I said in what I hoped was a voice conveying deep tragedy.

I leaned out of the open window and breathed in the glorious scent of just-turned hay. Sam, his pixie-like face grim with effort, was kicking a football in the apple orchard with one of his scruffy friends. Tiny, our Jack Russell terrier, yapped furiously as she chased after the ball. The early evening sky was an orangy-pink and a slight heat haze was starting to form in the distant fields, making Dad's cows melt into the background. There was nothing for miles around – except in one corner where the shiny new tiles of the Lynch mansion were visible through a clump of willows.

'I'll get Dad to plant a few more trees to hide it,' I thought.

'What's new?' asked Maggie, bounding in with her mouth full. She had grabbed an apple from the fruit-bowl on the way up.

'It's about the show in Athenry. Piggy made a mess of his canter leads again today – I swear he knows how much this show means to me. And then that awful Kelly Lynch and her sidekick Brenda saw me goof up my figure-of-eight and started laughing. It was the worst.'

'What of it! Ye'll be fine on the day.' Maggie was an incurable optimist.

'Kelly's bound to win on Moonstepper,' I said gloomily. 'And everyone will say it's because I'm not good enough to ride Piggy. He was always placed in the shows last summer. He'll get nowhere with me this year.'

'Kelly won't be winnin' no class. There'll be at least ten others there, including me and Rambo.'

'You?' I was very fond of Maggie but she just didn't make it at shows. She was always letting Rambo, her brother's ill-tempered pony, crash through fences or run out of the ring, or knock over the judge. Once he even upscuttled the refreshment tent.

'Oh, stuff it! There's more to life than horses. Do ye like me new shirt?' She twirled in front of me with more spirit than style. But then she didn't have a model's figure. In fact, she had no figure at all. She was short and plump. Her new tee-shirt revealed a ripple or two of flesh above the waist of her tight-fitting jeans. But she didn't seem to notice; or if she did she didn't care. Life to Maggie O'Connor was more than clothes or horses.

I got up slowly from the bed and looked at myself in the small mirror hanging beside the wardrobe. I was glad to be tall and slim; people said I had my mother's long legs. I have straight hair that comes half way down my back, brown in colour, that I tie back in a single plait. My eyes are green and wide-set and my smile is just a small bit crooked. At times I try to correct it by standing for hours in front of the mirror, pulling down one side of my face. Then I forget about it – until the next time I catch sight of myself in some car's rear-view mirror.

'Let's go and check on Piggy,' I said. 'He may need more water.'

'Tea first,' said Maggie firmly.

I always loved to come down to the kitchen, with its cosy terracotta tiles and huge dresser stacked with plates and cups and jugs. Warm from the Aga range, it was usually full of enticing smells like bread being baked or jam simmering or fruit being bottled. It opened into a large sitting-room that ran the full length of the farmhouse. Tonight, even though it was warm outside, a small fire flickered cheerfully at the far end of the timber-floored room. The high-arched stone fireplace that surrounded it was tall enough for me to stand up in. When I was very small Dad used to tell me Santa would never have the slightest trouble coming down it.

Tea wasn't quite ready. Dad was just clearing away some papers from the table, so Maggie and I helped

Mom to set it. I was surprised to see John Moran there. He's our local vet, a small wiry man, well able to catch and hold even the most contrary cow. He usually didn't drop in without a reason. Had something happened?

'Anything wrong?' I asked. With fifty odd cows and calves, not to mention the horses, it seemed some animal was always sick or injured.

'No, nothing wrong with the stock,' assured Dad. I thought his voice sounded a trifle strained.

'Nothing at all, Clare,' said Mom, almost in the same breath.

Maggie and I helped her to arrange plates of cold

ham, chutney, coleslaw and brown scones – I could have sworn I smelled rashers frying.

'Ye bake the nicest scones, Mrs Fox,' praised Maggie. 'Mam is hopeless at baking. Her scones are always hard as rocks.'

'Maybe you should give her a hand,' said Mom in an abstracted way. Maggie's mother taught and didn't have a lot of time for baking.

Sam raced in with Tiny at his feet, and plonked himself down in the nearest chair. But before he could take a scone, Mom asked wearily, 'Did you wash your hands?'

Of course he hadn't, so off he went. 'Give your hair a brush,' I called after him. I always envied him his blond hair, especially in summer. It went so well with a tan.

'Apple-cake and cream, anyone?' asked Mom, after we had finished our plates of cold meat. Maggie held up an empty side-plate.

'You'd better watch it,' I warned. 'If you eat much more poor Rambo will collapse under you.'

Looking back on it, if Maggie hadn't been there it would have been a pretty dismal tea. Mom and Dad said little. John Moran, who was always good for a story or a joke, whether animal or human, was equally silent.

I stole a guilty glance at Dad. Maybe he was annoyed at my outburst earlier. But there was no reproachful look when no one was looking – the usual put-down. He just looked worried.

Anyway, Mags and I carried the conversation, with

Sam making the odd wisecrack. We talked about the coming show, who would be riding in our class, and how good their ponies were. We talked about Piggy and Rambo and how much training we should do with them during the week. We discussed Kelly and her fabulous new pony. And her family. Her mother always wore fancy clothes with short skirts and gobs of gold jewellery. I loved to watch her make her way across a sodden field wearing high heels.

In the sweet-scented evening, Maggie and I, locked arm and arm, went out to see Piggy. Maggie sniffed the air. 'Better than any any French perfume,' she said, taking long steps to the stable.

Once inside, putting my arms around Piggy and giving him his apple, I nodded. I felt good again. The whole summer lay ahead. Suddenly I was sure I could get Piggy right. Maybe I could even get a place at Athenry.

But in bed that night the uneasiness returned. Was there something wrong?

I decided to say nothing about the new jodhpurs to Mom and Dad.

3 Off to the Show

'Clare, go to bed!' Mom ordered when she saw my bare legs creeping down the back stairs. 'You'll never get up in time for the show tomorrow.'

'Mom, I can't sleep,' I complained. 'I'm all jittery inside. What if I forget the course and jump the wrong fences.'

'What of it!' she reassured. 'Remember, shows are supposed to be fun.'

'Can I just watch you for a moment?' I begged. 'Then I'll go straight back to bed.'

She gave me a dark look. 'You sure will!' But she didn't insist I go back at once and I sat down next to Tiny in the old armchair beside the fire, feet tucked up under me. Rex, who lay curled up on an old mat in the corner of the kitchen, flapped his tail in greeting, too comfortable to raise his head.

Mom was tall and pretty with a wide smile and an unhurried way of doing everything. I loved watching her as she made preparations for the picnic lunch we always had at shows.

First she made a box of sandwiches for the grown-ups, full of ham, tomato, onion and spicy mustard. Then she made a box of plain sandwiches for the children – our favourite was ham. Next she filled an empty biscuit-tin with fairy cakes iced with dark chocolate. All this was carefully packed into the large hamper open on the chair beside her. A bag of red apples and small packets of crisps were tucked into any spaces. Now for the drinks. Two large flasks filled with hot water for coffee and tea, a jug of orange and one of milk, were put into a separate carrying bag.

By this time the kitchen clock stood at ten to midnight. Mom snapped off the light, let the dogs out, and chased me up the back stairs to bed.

Streaks of sunlight stole through my bedroom curtains and danced upon the picture of Red Rum pinned to my bedroom wall. Through the open window I could hear the sounds of early morning – a cock crowing, hens clucking about their newly laid eggs, cows lowing.

Suddenly I sat up with a start. I had just 're-membered what day it was.

'Mom! Dad! Sam! Anybody! What time is it?' I yelled frantically. The house was silent except for the high-pitched beeping of an electronic game. I raced into Sam's room across the hall.

'Sam, what time it is? Have I missed the show?'

Sam was lying on his back in bed, blond head propped up on three pillows, pushing buttons meth-odically.

'Look at a clock,' he yawned.

'Thanks a lot,' I shouted as I dashed out of his room and down the back stairs.

'Please, God, let it be early,' I prayed out loud, almost not daring to look at the kitchen clock. My heart lifted when I saw that it was only twenty minutes to eight.

'Morning, angel,' Dad called from the living-room. He was peering out of the front window at three brood mares who were grazing in the aftergrass with their foals. The sky promised another hot dry day.

'Gonna be a grand day. Are you ready for the show?' he asked, walking back towards the kitchen.

'Dad, I feel sick,' I answered with my head in my hands. 'I don't think I'll be able to ride.'

'After a bowl of cornflakes you'll be fine. Now run up and get some clothes on and find Mom. I'll start breakfast. Tell Sam I want him.'

Five minutes later, dressed in jeans and a tee-shirt, I ran outside to look for Mom. I knew she would be washing and plaiting Piggy.

'Mom, Dad says to come in for breakfast,' I called when I found her and Piggy in the back yard. Piggy was tied to a fence post, his just-washed coat drying in the sun.

'I'll only be a tic. I want to finish off plaiting,' she said.

She had carefully divided Piggy's mane into seven even bunches of hair (eight including the forelock), measuring each section with the mane-comb. She then plaited each before turning it under twice and securing it with a plaiting band.

'He looks gorgeous! Thanks, Mom,' I said, putting my arms around his wet neck.

Have I described Piggy? Perhaps this is the right moment. He is twelve hands (a hand is four inches), two inches high. He is the colour of dark cream, the kind you get in very rich Jersey milk, with a black mane and tail. He has four black legs, a big solid neck, and a wide back to sit on. He also has a huge belly – hence his nickname. Now, thanks to Mom, he looked really smart.

Breakfast was a flurry of plates banging, cutlery clinking, chairs scraping and voices buzzing. I don't remember eating anything.

My mouth felt like cotton wool and my stomach felt all fluttery. I pushed away my plate and rushed upstairs to change.

'Clare, do hurry up!' Mom's voice from below, ten minutes later, sounded irritated.

When I got down, she was busy packing my well-oiled saddle, bridle and girth into a large cardboard box which was padded with Piggy's light stable-rug. 'Check the bags for your other riding things. Make sure your hat, gloves and whip are packed.'

'Mom, where's my tie-pin?' I was rooting through the contents of one of the bags.

'I've no idea, but this isn't the time to start looking for it. We need to get the jeep loaded now.'

'But, Mom, I need it. It's my good-luck pin,' I pleaded.

'Where do you think it is?'

I stood in the middle of the kitchen, dressed like a champion in my light-blue riding-shirt, tie, tan jodhpurs clipped neatly over my black jodhpur boots, hair pulled into a long braid down my back. My navy riding-coat was in a dress bag; my black

cap, brown gloves and whip were packed. But I didn't feel like a champion.

'How much is the pin worth to you?' I heard Sam's greedy voice ask.

'You brat! Where did you find it?' I yelled when I saw him holding the pin in his grimy hand outside the kitchen door.

'Thank goodness. Now let's get the bags loaded.' Mom sounded relieved. Outside, the old jeep was hitched to the horse-box. Piggy was already inside.

We were on our way to Athenry Show. Sam was totally absorbed in making faces at any passers-by, while I listened with half an ear to Mom and Dad talking.

Dad was born and raised on the farm in the days when work in the fields was more important than school lessons. He wasn't too tall. Stocky build. Face and hands reddened by constant exposure to weather. Piercing blue eyes, always half hidden under the brim of a cap. Our farm was mainly suckler cows but Dad also kept a few mares for breeding. He loved horses since the days when he had helped his father to drive a team of work horses. Now our horses were kept for pleasure, for quiet rides down the back roads or a fast gallop across the fields.

'Are we almost there?' I asked, feeling anxious and excited at the same time. One part of me wanted to get there and get it over with. The other half hoped we would never arrive.

'Just about. Why don't you look out for the show signs? It's a new location this year.' Mom sounded a bit on edge. Worried about me and Piggy, I supposed.

'Can I have some money to buy a watch?' asked Sam.

Sam was hopeless. He hadn't a screed of interest in horses or ponies. He just went to the shows for the picnic lunch, the odd souvenir he got free and any sweets he could scrounge.

'No, and don't be hanging around the traders' tents, d'you hear?' Dad warned as he slowed the jeep down behind a line of lorries and horse-boxes. 'Here

we are, along with the rest of the county,' he sighed,
looking at the length of the queue.

July was the month when the shows were in full
swing, with at least one every week-end. They
weren't just about horses and ponies. There were
competitions for the best cows and sheep, a dog
show and a bonny baby contest, prizes for home-
made breads and cakes, as well as for home-grown
fruits and vegetables. Men competed at a sheaf
throw or a tug-or-war, there was a fun fair for the
children, and a tea-tent for the old people and
anyone else who just wanted to sit down.

Hail, rain and snow didn't matter. The show went
on regardless. But then we were used to rain in the
west. One of our favourite jokes was about the
tourist who asked what the weather prospects were
and was told: 'If you can see the mountains, it's
going to rain; if you can't see them, it's raining.'

But today at Athenry Show, it promised to be a
really fine day.

4 Athenry

'I feel awful, Maggie. I'm going to be sick or faint, or both, in the middle of the ring,' I moaned. 'I told Mom and Dad I wasn't able.'

Taking full advantage of my divided attention, Piggy grabbed the chance to drop his head for a nibble of sweet grass underfoot. The sudden jerk on my reins pulled me out of the saddle and almost on to the ground.

'Stop it, Piggy, please stop it,' I begged, blinking back tears. Piggy continued to graze greedily. Totally indifferent.

'Stop messin', Clare,' commanded Maggie. 'Give him a good wallop with yer whip and *make* him stand up.'

I obeyed her and finally managed to get his head up from the grass. I couldn't say anything. A large lump seemed to have formed in my throat.

'We'll go down to the practice ring and warm up. We need to make sure they're on their toes. Are ye right?' She kicked Rambo's sides vigorously until he slowly moved forward. I followed behind.

Maggie was dressed in a wool jacket that had once belonged to her older brother. It had been part of his confirmation suit, now out of fashion, doomed to hang idly in an O'Connor wardrobe until Maggie resurrected it. The rest of her outfit was inherited from a cousin – knee-high, black rubber riding-boots, and a pair of jodhpurs which needed the help of several cunningly placed pins to ease the strain on her waistband. She had also got the loan of a jockey's skull-cap, the type worn on racetracks. With bright red hair flying behind, she looked a million dollars.

I wished I did. All I was conscious of were my dreadful jodhpurs. Though at least my black velvet riding-hat, last year's surprise gift from Santa, couldn't be faulted.

Maggie and I rode Rambo and Piggy to the warm-up ring where five or six riders and ponies were trotting and cantering around the small roped-in area. A practice fence had been set up in the middle but Maggie and I chose just to trot slowly around the outermost edge, avoiding the queue for it.

'How are the Dynamic Duo on their turbo-charged hobby-horses?' laughed Kelly Lynch as she rode up beside us on Moonstepper.

The two of them were outfitted impeccably. Kelly in a slate-blue tweed jacket, unmistakably custom-made, beige jodhpurs, brown jodhpur boots, and a brown velvet riding-hat. A dazzling white stock-tie and brown leather gloves completed what you could only call an ensemble. Her thick blonde hair was tied back with a beige and brown striped ribbon.

Moonstepper was fitted out in well-oiled English tack, saddle and bridle gleaming against his smooth muscled body and chiselled face. His mane was divided up into countless tiny plaits and his tail was pulled back into an elegant single braid.

'See you in the winners' circle,' said Kelly, raising her whip in a derisive salute. Then she turned her pony abruptly and took the practice fence in three strides, leaving feet between Moonstepper and the top rail. I stared in awe.

'Hasn't the little rap got some neck?' said Maggie, refusing to be impressed. 'I'd like to see that one brought down a notch or two, ye know.'

The loudspeaker gave a couple of groans, then a loud shriek, before it announced: 'We are now ready to start the Working Hunter Pony Class 133. Riders may inspect the course mounted. Please do so without delay. The judge is ready to start.'

My heart sank and my chest heaved. Will I ever get through this nightmare? I wondered, only to have a voice break in on my thoughts. Mom was coming quickly towards me. 'I'll walk the course with both of you. Hurry, we haven't much time.'

Mom knew very little about pony jumping or show competition. But this didn't phase her in the slightest – she was used to overcoming obstacles. She grew up in a city and knew nothing about farming when she married Dad. She learned everything from a book or from watching the experts. Now she could drive a tractor, milk a cow, plant, harvest, can or pickle any fruit or vegetable. A Working Hunter Pony class was all in a day's work.

Already riders on their ponies were walking from fence to fence when Mom, Maggie and I entered the ring. Nine numbered fences were arranged in a course which included several changes of direction and a two-part jump called a double. All were natural, many typical of what you would find when riding across country. Maximum height and width – two foot, six inches.

'Clare, look at number one,' cried Maggie as she trotted Rambo up to the first fence. 'That's a cinch, isn't it?' About two foot high, made of plain timber rails with pieces of evergreen intertwined, the effect was a small and inviting bush fence.

Mom had already walked down to the second fence and was inspecting the width of it when we got there on Piggy and Rambo.

'It's fine, girls. The hay bales make it look wide but it isn't really,' she encouraged. 'Just remember how easy it was to jump the tyres on a pole at home. No problem here.'

'Will ye look over there?' screeched Maggie, pointing to a fence at the other end of the ring. 'That's a blooming cottage we've got to jump. Can ye believe it?'

'Mags, you're going the wrong way,' I hissed at her. 'We have to go round the course in order. We need to look at number three.'

The third fence, a simple wooden gate standing about two and a half foot high, looked tall because of its narrow design. My heart began to pound when I rode Piggy close to it.

Maggie was still gawking at the miniature cottage, fence four. Even Mom looked worried as she walked around the white-washed wooden structure with the newly thatched roof. Its shiny red door and green-

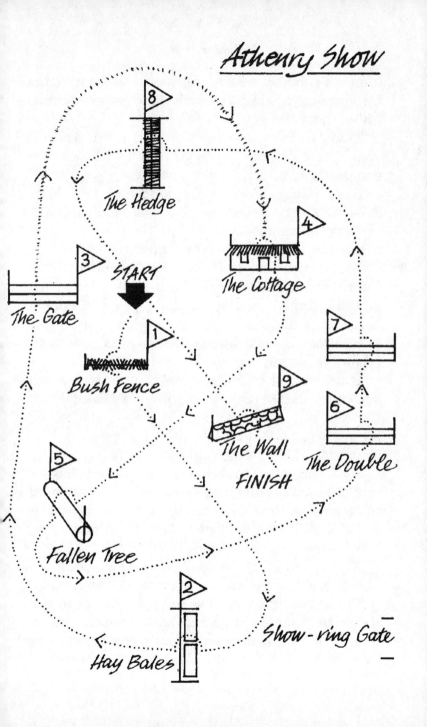

trimmed windows made Piggy shy away from it, and Maggie was finding it equally hard to get Rambo within thirty feet of it.

'Mom, I can't. I just can't do it,' I cried, defeated even before I began. 'Let's go back to the box. I'm not able.' My throat began to make gulping sounds.

'Hush, Clare, don't make a scene,' said Mom sharply. 'Just do your best. That's all your dad and I ever ask from you.'

Mom was not going to let me quit.

Maggie was still trying to get Rambo past the cottage as Mom and I checked the fallen tree, fence five, and turned towards the sloping parallel double, fences six and seven.

'Just pace it,' said Mom, 'so you get a good take-off for the second part.'

At this point I could have looked at a six-foot wall and not reacted any differently. My confidence, flimsy at best, was gone. The fences were far too big for me to jump. I knew I would fail. It would only be a question of how soon. And how painfully.

The loudspeaker squawked again: 'Please clear the ring. The class must now begin. Give your number to the ring steward. Thank you.'

'Let's go,' I said without feeling. I was numb with fear.

'We need to see the hedge,' Mom called unmoved, already walking past the exiting riders to fence eight.

'Please clear the ring. The judge is anxious to start this class,' the loudspeaker barked again. As we joined the last of the ponies and riders to leave the ring, we passed by the stone wall, fence nine.

At the entrance gate to the ring, the steward was asking what order we wanted to jump in. Kelly had already taken the first spot. Maggie put in for fourth, and I followed at fifth.

Brenda Fahy was standing next to Kelly on Moonstepper, rubbing his already glistening black coat. Talk about a toady! Why did Kelly bother with her? I looked down at Piggy's coat; it was clean and shiny but nothing like Moonstepper's.

As we stood there I felt I was about to be given a cold shower. Ice cold. I hate cold showers.

5 Disaster!

'Number one, when you are ready,' the ring steward called as he opened the gate. Kelly turned her head and looked in our direction before heading into the ring. Another cackle from the loudspeaker: 'Kelly Lynch, riding Moonstepper, is our first competitor.'

Kelly let Moonstepper do an extended trot into the centre of the ring. Why couldn't I get Piggy to do that flashing footwork? It just wasn't fair. She paused in front of the judge and bowed dramatically. After the judge said a few words to her, she wheeled around to make her approach to the first fence. What an entrance!

Moonstepper was anxious to gallop but Kelly kept him checked to a canter. They sailed over each of the nine fences, making them look small and easy. Then she again bowed graciously to the judge before leaving the ring. Without saying a word to any of us, she trotted off towards her father's horse-box.

'Ain't she the little witch?' Maggie growled. 'She sure as heck don't deserve that good pony! Rambo and I will show her a trick or two, won't we, fella?' She patted her sour-looking pony.

'Number four, please,' the ring steward beckoned as the third rider and pony trotted back to the gate.

Maggie started kicking Rambo's sides to get him into the ring but Rambo had no intention of leaving

Piggy and the other ponies. He stood glued to the ground despite all Maggie's kicking and slapping with her whip. The ring steward, assessing the situation, grabbed him by the bridle and led him in.

Maggie did a swooping type of bow to the judge as well as to the crowd; clearly she was going to enjoy her time in the limelight. If she ever got started, that was. After a few words from the judge, she resumed her furious kicking to try and to get Rambo to walk forward, but the judge had to wave her hat at him before he trotted forward reluctantly. Maggie turned him at the top of the ring and headed for fence one. Rambo, much to my surprise and probably everyone else's jumped it beautifully.

Maggie cantered towards the exit gate, then tried to turn him to approach fence two. But Rambo had different ideas. He wouldn't turn. Maggie adopted a bracing position, her two feet stuck in front of the girth, her body hauling back on the reins with all her might. Rambo resisted, stuck up his head and pulled back. The tug of war lasted only seconds. Rambo, the victor, charged out through the exit gate, scattering ponies, riders and officials, as he headed for the group of ponies he had just left.

'Number four has, unfortunately, been eliminated,' wheezed the loudspeaker. 'Maggie O'Connor on Rambo. Eliminated.'

'Tough luck, Mags,' I said as Rambo slid in next to Piggy.

'He's very green. I told that to the lady. But did ye see us fly the jump? It was the best. I bet I get a better score than Kelly on that one!' Trust Maggie to snatch victory from the jaws of defeat.

'Number five! Quickly! The judge is waiting.'

I dug in my heels but Piggy balked. He was about to do a Rambo. But the steward was quick to give him a sharp smack on the rump to change his mind. I caught Mom's eye as I entered the ring. She gave me the crossed-finger sign for luck. I trotted up to the judge, hands shaking, breathing fast and shallow. I halted and remembered to bow my head and drop my hand in salute.

'Name and number,' the judge asked, smiling at me.

My voice squeaked before I found the words.

'Do you know the course?'

'Yes, Ma'am,' in a very small voice.

'Go ahead then,' said the judge.

I turned Piggy and trotted towards the top of the ring. I pushed him into a canter and we headed for the small bush fence. He took it without hesitation and cantered on strongly. I could feel his body veering towards the exit gate but the ring steward was there in the gap, fanning his programme as a deterrent. Piggy took the hint and we headed towards the hay-bale fence. Again he jumped it smoothly but sooner than I had expected, and I lost one of my stirrups on landing. I tried to hold his mane while I wriggled my foot around searching for it. At last I felt the clunk of it on my foot, but only in time to see the gate looming up. My heart screamed 'No' but Piggy just sailed over it.

His big lift-off again sent me flying up on his neck. In trying to regain my position this time, my mind sort of blanked out and I lost track of the fence numbers. Then I remembered Maggie's cottage. I turned just in time to see it in full view. Piggy saw the red door and the green-trimmed windows and swung to the left, towards the exit gate.

The steward again flicked his programme to block him and we slowed to a trot. I heard a voice – it must have been Mom's – shouting, 'Give him a good sharp slap and shorten up your reins. You can do it, sweetheart.'

I trotted back up to the top of the ring and headed once more for the cottage. Piggy paused, but with checked reins he had nowhere to go except up and over. His enormous leap unseated me and I landed on his neck. Again! I heard the crowd gasp. I don't remember how I wiggled back into the saddle but I did. Then I heard Mom's voice, 'The fallen tree. And then the double.'

I was so shaken up by my near fall that I responded without thinking. Actually both were easy to jump after the huge cat-leap at the cottage. Now I had only two fences to jump. A surge of courage went through me. I knew I could do it! At fence eight, I grabbed a bit of Piggy's mane to help to steady me while he jumped. The result was better; at least I landed in the saddle.

I wasn't afraid of fence nine. Piggy and I were used to stone walls – the farm had nothing but walls criss-crossing it. He jumped it beautifully and for the first time I stayed with him. I was almost pleased with myself as I headed for the gate. Mom was standing to one side of it.

'Clare, go back and salute the judge,' she called out. I smiled at her, half in a daze. I didn't really hear what she was saying.

'Clare, turn Piggy around and go back to the judge.' Her voice was much louder this time and the message sank in. I suddenly remembered that after jumping the course each rider must return to the judge and salute before leaving the ring. I walked Piggy back, halted and saluted. The judge said nothing but she smiled and nodded.

The loudspeaker gave a squeal: 'That was number five, Clare Fox.'

Mom was still at the gate, Maggie and Rambo close behind.

'Mom, I told you my lucky pin would work. I told you,' I sang out, not able to contain my excitement.

'Ye're the best, ye know,' said Maggie, thrilled by my good fortune, not in the least put out by her early exit.

'Great stuff,' said Dad from the back of the gallery.

Sam, dripping ice-cream in hand, wandered up and patted Piggy. 'Will you get a prize?' He pointed a sticky finger in the direction of the tea-tent. 'Get a load of that.'

Mom, Maggie and I turned and stared. Beyond a clump of trees, a woman was putting a pony that looked like Moonstepper through his paces. I recognised her: Mrs Burke who had a riding-school near Ennis, the one who was coaching Kelly. The pony was cantering the figure-of-eight in perfect style and formation. I groaned.

'Dad, go over and see if it's Moonstepper?'

'What does that matter?' asked Mom. 'If you're called back, concentrate on Piggy. Don't mind the others.'

'Sure.' But my moment of glory was fading fast.

As Dad walked over towards the trees, a man approached him. It looked like Kelly's father, Con Lynch. Dad seemed to stiffen up. They had a few words together. It seemed to me that Mr Lynch was doing most of the talking. Then he turned and went over to Mrs Burke and the pony. So it *was* Moon-stepper.

'What was that about?' I asked.

'Nothing,' said Dad. 'Nothing really... he just wanted to know how you had done.'

Mr Lynch? Me? That wasn't the answer. Probably on about Sam kicking balls into his rose-garden or the cows taking a short cut over his lawn. Our grazing fields were on the other side of the Lynch mansion and the cows crossed over to them through a rough piece of ground that lay between their land and the river.

'Can I get a lemonade? I'm dying,' begged Sam, clutching his throat.

The loudspeaker crackled alive: 'Will the following please return to the ring – one, seven, nine, three, two and five.'

'Yes!' I squealed, confidence coming back in a flash.

In the ring the judge's assistant asked us to line up in the order we were called. Standing quietly at the end of the line I watched as the other riders performed. Kelly went first. Perfect. Everything. And a figure-of-eight you'd die for. Confidence ebbing, I tried to plan out where I would start my circles. My heart was pounding and my fingers were shaking when the assistant finally called out, 'Number five.' It was my turn.

Slowly I walked Piggy up to the judge. I halted before saluting.

'Please walk your pony forward and then trot back to me,' the judge directed. 'Do you know your test?'

I nodded.

'Then you may start.'

I did my best to walk forward in a straight line. At least I hoped it was straight, though Piggy kept veering slightly to the right. When it came to the trotting back, he began slowly and didn't pick up speed. I felt as if we were ploughing through deep mud.

Worried about the poor showing we were making, I got completely confused as I headed off for my figure-of-eight. I think I did the same direction for both circles, so it wasn't really a figure-of-eight at all. I was so relieved to get to the gallop stage that I kicked Piggy into a wild charge. I returned to the line, puffed from our race around the ring, hoping the last bit would make up for my wonky circles. The ring assistant reminded me to go and salute the judge once more.

The feeling of gloom returned as she asked us to walk around the ring. I knew I had made a mess of my figure-of-eight: wrong direction, wrong leads, crooked circles, rotten everything. I couldn't walk, trot or canter. Now all I wanted was to get out of that stupid ring.

'I hate riding,' I said to myself. 'Why do I do it? I should just give up and let the Kelly Lynchs of the world take over.'

My eye strayed to the railing. Our vet, John Moran, was standing there. He smiled and waved. His nephew, Nick Moran, was beside him. He lives in County Meath but for the last two summers he had come to Galway to help his uncle in his animal clinic. I looked away. I didn't need any more humiliation.

The results were being announced over the loudspeaker:

'Will you please line up according to the numbers called? Numbers one, three, seven, two, nine and five.'

Last place! My worst nightmare was a reality. As I followed the other riders to the centre of the ring to form a line, I wished Mom and Dad, John and Nick, Maggie and Brenda, and anyone else who knew me, would disappear into the ground.

'Well done!' The judge interrupted my thoughts. She handed me a white consolation ribbon. For what? Not falling off? Not doing a Maggie and Rambo and disappearing after the first fence? I stuffed it into my pocket.

'You need to practise your individual test,' the judge was saying in a kindly voice. 'Do you have anyone to help you?'

'No,' I whispered in a choked voice, trying to hold back the tears.

'Don't get upset about it,' she consoled. 'You're very lucky. Your pony is a true gentleman. You will learn the flat work in time.'

As we did a victory round before leaving the ring, my feeling of failure left me for a moment as the warm July breeze blew in my face. I leaned forward, taking my weight off Piggy's back as we galloped.

6 Nick

Mom and Dad were talking to John and Nick when I rode out of the ring. I felt my right foot jammed painfully from behind.

'Oink, oink!' Kelly was holding her nose as she headed past, towards her father's car. 'I thought all farmyard animals belonged in pens.'

I looked around, hoping no one had heard her. But Nick had. He raised his eyebrows and whispered, 'Who was that?'

'Well done, Clare, aren't you pleased?' Mom praised, giving Piggy a slice of apple. 'What did the judge say?'

'Good work,' said Dad. He gave me a vague pat on the shoulder. 'Now, take Piggy back to the box. I want to get home and see if that fertilizer has been delivered. Nick, be a good lad and give Clare a hand. Now where's that brother of yours.'

'You rode well,' said Nick politely, as we walked towards our jeep and horse-box. He was almost as tall as Dad but very thin and bony. His hands and arms looked like a cartoon sketch the way they stuck out of his polo shirt. He had shaggy brown hair that hung over his ears and across one eye. Blue eyes. Bright blue.

I untacked Piggy and put on his canvas head-collar. Nick let down the ramp and waited until I had

Piggy loaded inside before closing it. He opened the jockey door so that I could get out. Then he picked up my bridle and saddle and put them into the back of the jeep.

'Thanks,' I muttered awkwardly. I wasn't used to having older boys around, especially ones who treated me like a grown-up.

'Who was the girl on the black pony?' he enquired as he leaned against the side of the jeep.

'Kelly Lynch,' I mumbled. I never wanted to hear her name again.

'Is she always so mean to you?'

'Yes, she picks on me a lot.'

'Why?'

'She thinks I'm a punk rider. On a punk pony. She knows she's better than I am. And it's true. She's a better rider, and she has a brilliant pony. She always gets first or second at shows.'

'That should make her very happy. There must be some other reason. Is she at your school?'

'She's in the class behind. She's only there until she goes to some swank boarding-school.'

'That's probably it. Feels you're too brainy.'

I stared at him. *Kelly Lynch!* The girl who had everything? What did she care about school? I said nothing.

'Clare,' Nick's runners were tracing a pattern in the dust at his feet, 'who helps you to train?'

'Nobody. Mom and Dad aren't really into showing. They ride but they don't know much about training and competitions and things like that.'

'It's a pity. You have the makings of a good rider.'

'Me?' I stared at him.

He stared back, then said jokingly, 'But do you always ride on your pony's neck?'

'What do you mean?'

'You managed to land on your pony's neck after every fence you jumped. It was a miracle you didn't fall off.'

I decided to change the subject. 'The judge liked only the dark-coloured ponies. Piggy didn't have a chance.'

'Clare, Piggy's colour had nothing to do with the judging. You were placed last in the second part because you were the worst rider, with an out of condition pony who wouldn't obey you.'

Nick looked me straight in the eye.

'How dare you say that about Piggy! I might be the world's worst rider but Piggy is a super pony. He won all sorts of rosettes last summer.'

'But this is *this* summer – and he's fat and flabby. And disobedient.'

'I knew I shouldn't ride at the show.' My voice began to crack. 'I only did it for Mom and Dad. And look where it's got me. I let them down. I let Piggy down. I let everybody down.' I was about to burst into tears.

'Crying won't solve anything,' said Nick seriously. 'If you're a lousy rider – you said it, I didn't – learn to ride. If Piggy is fat and out of shape, get him fit.'

'Sure! It's easy for you to say so, but lessons and training take money. A lot of it.'

'Not if you take me on,' said Nick.

'You?'

'I did quite a lot of competing in Meath. Before I got too tall for ponies.'

'I'd only be wasting your time. I'm a crummy rider. And Piggy can be as thick as they come.'

'I wouldn't offer to help if I didn't think you could do it. Piggy's the ideal hunter pony. Only needs to be schooled. And at least you managed to stay on his back – which is rule number one. A few lessons would sort out your jumping and your individual test. Are you on?'

'You won't have the time.'

Did I really want to spend the whole summer training a stupid pony? And trying to please Nick. He'd be a tough teacher. I could see that.

'But I will. Uncle John isn't doing so much small animal work now and I haven't graduated to horses and cattle yet. Think it over. Maybe we could give Kelly Lynch something to really think about.'

That did it. Could there be anything in the whole wide world to equal beating Kelly Lynch?

Nick sensed my change of heart.

'Then we're partners?' He smiled and held out his hand.

'Partners,' I agreed and gripped it tightly.

'Clare and Nick, Sitting in a tree, K-i-s-s-i-n-g,' a voice from within the horse-box chanted.

'Sam, I'm going to kill you,' I shouted. Younger brothers are a pain.

Nick laughed. 'Little pitchers have big ears. Come on out of there and I'll clobber you.'

7 Country Blues

All through supper – my favourite this time – I babbled away about my plans. Nick was coming over in the morning. Nick and I would get the figure-of-eight right. Nick was to show me how to give Piggy the correct signs so that he wouldn't get his canter leads mixed up. Nick was going to teach me to jump without landing on Piggy's neck every time.

'Sounds like the answer to the show-jumper's prayer,' grunted Dad.

Mom looked glum. I knew what she was thinking. Clare! Up in the air for five minutes. Down in the dumps for the next five hours. Well, I was determined to show her. Kelly Lynch had a fight on her hands.

That reminded me. 'Dad, what were you and Mr Lynch talking about at the show? Don't tell me it was me. He doesn't even know I exist.'

Dad and Mom looked at each other.

'I suppose you'd better tell them,' said Mom.

'I suppose so.' Dad looked over at me.

My mouth felt dry. 'What is it?' It had to be something terrible. Mom and Dad took most things in their stride. 'Never trouble trouble until trouble troubles you,' was another of Dad's favourites.

Mom, who had started to get up for something, sat down again.

'Remember last Tuesday when you came in and I was at the table reading a letter,' began Dad.

'Yeah.' I did remember. I had thought it strange to see him home at that hour.

'The letter was from Con Lynch's solicitor. O'Neill had it sent over to me.' Gerard O'Neill was our solicitor.

'He's bought our farm,' whispered Sam. 'He's going to turn us out.' He'd been hearing too many stories at school about the evictions in the olden days.

'You know the field we call the duck-pond – where the cattle cross over into the grazing fields.'

'Of course!' I was ready to explode with impatience. Since I was knee-high to a sparrow I'd been helping Dad or Mom to drive the cows over that meadow into our fields on the other side of what was now Con Lynch's land. Not much lately because of school and riding Piggy but the duck-pond meadow was part of our life.

'Mr Lynch doesn't want us to cross the cattle through that field any more.'

'But surely he can't stop it. We've done it for years.'

'He claims he owns it.'

'Does he?'

'I don't know for certain. O'Neill is checking it out.'

'We should have bought that land,' said Mom gloomily. 'I always felt it was stupid having our farm in two pieces.'

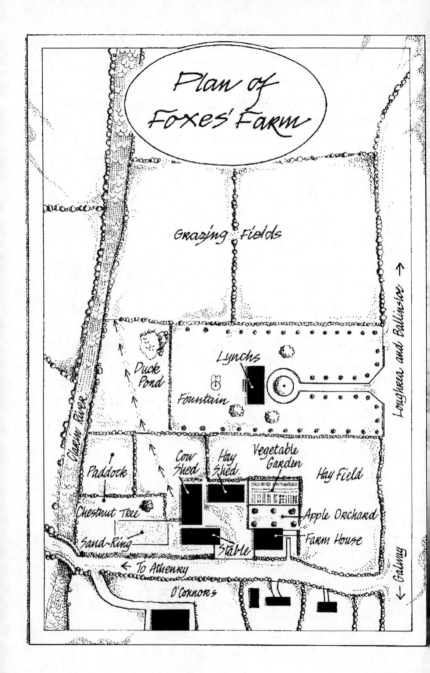

'But we didn't know it was for sale – it was a private sale.... Anyway, it probably isn't as bad as we think. We've always used that field for crossing the cattle. O'Neill feels we must have established a right of way.'

'What's that?'

'It means that if someone owns a piece of land, and you have always used it to get from one place to another, that right can't be taken away from you. You have what's called a right of way.'

'Well we can certainly prove it,' said Mom. 'I've used that meadow ever since I've been here and that's eleven years. How long does it take to establish a right of way?'

'Twenty years or thereabouts. We certainly qualify on that ground. My dad always used it.'

'Then what's the problem?' I was puzzled.

'I just have this feeling.' Dad continued to look worried. 'Con Lynch is a very smart man. He'd have the top legal advice. If he *does* own that meadow, maybe we don't have a right of way. We're the only people who use it, remember. Maybe he's found a loophole.'

'I don't believe it,' I said. 'He's just used to getting his own way. Riding over everyone. Like Kelly.'

'I hope so.'

'What happens now?' asked Mom.

'O'Neill is looking up old maps to see if the right of way is marked. Checking the deeds of the grazing fields to see if it's mentioned. And trying to establish if Lynch *does* own the meadow. That's why I asked

John Moran around that evening. I thought he might
have known something about that bit of land. But he
doesn't.'

'But what would happen if we didn't have the...
whatever it is?' Sam stumbled over the words.

'Every time we wanted to change the cattle, we'd
have to drive them along the main Dublin road.'

A motorway! Cars flashing past at sixty miles an
hour! Even I could see that that wouldn't work. And
there was no other way. The Clarin river bounded
the other side of the meadow.

'Where are you going, Dad?' I asked as he got up
from the table. Rex jumped to his feet, tail wagging.

'Out. I need to get some air.' Leaning against the
back of the chair, he looked worn and beaten.

'Can I come?' I wanted to be with him. I knew
how much the farm meant to him. He loved his land,
always spoke about the cows and calves with pride.
He was forever telling us stories about helping his
father and grandfather. Now he might lose it all,
because of a greedy neighbour

'Sure, girleen.'

We took our plates and mugs to the sink. Mom
remained sitting, a mug of tea poised between her
hands. Sam, for once, was silent. He was busy slicing
apples, bananas, pears and oranges on to his side-
plate, trying to copy the fruit-salad cup for sale today
at the show. Mom was too deep in thought to notice
the drippy mess of peels and seeds that were falling
all over her clean cotton tablecloth.

Dad grabbed two ash sticks left in the corner of the

utility room before heading outside. It was a strict rule that we must always carry a stick when crossing land; a farm animal can turn into a dangerous beast at any time. As we headed across the yard to the hay shed, I took Dad's hand. The warm smell of a summer evening mixed with the sweet smell of new hay. Dad buried his hand deep into a stacked bale to check it for heat – hay that is baled too early or while still damp heats up within and turns the bale mouldy. Having checked three or four, he gave me a nod of approval and we set off again.

This time we headed across the back paddock, taking the crooked path the cows had worn through the centre of the small enclosed field. I used my stick as a scythe, knocking off the purple heads of the pesty thistles. My eyes scanned the outer edges of the field laced with wild flowers of every colour. When we reached the gate to the meadow Dad didn't bother opening it. He stepped up on the first bar and swung his long legs, one and then the other, over the top. I had to climb three bars to do the same.

'Dad, can they really stop us from crossing here?' I asked. The well-trodden path continued to slope across the field.

'I don't know, but Lynch is sure going to try.'

We walked on silently, sticks in hand, across the narrow stretch of land. A small duck-pond, almost half dried up by the summer heat, lay to our right. The river Clarin, also dried well below the banks, lay to our left. We reached the far gate and paused for a time, looking at the grazing cows and calves.

I climbed up to sit on the top bar.

'Did I ever tell you...?' Dad was looking at the duck-pond.

'No!' (This was always our prelude to the telling of a story.)

'When I was a lad about your age, I used to spend most of my time here. Old Paddy Gallagher – he was the man who sold the grazing fields to my dad – used to live in a small cottage over there,' pointing in the direction of the Lynch mansion. 'He stayed there after his brothers and sisters left, taking care of his father and mother. After they died, he continued to live there alone and work their land.

'One day he asked me if I would like a job. He wanted to rear ducks and sell their eggs in the local shops. The problem was that ducks are water-birds and need a pond. But he had an idea. There was an abandoned well just below that outcrop of rock, with steps down to it. He figured that if he opened up the sides of the well and pushed them back the natural spring would fill it and make a small pond. It would take time since he only had a spade, a pick, a loy and a wheelbarrow. But he couldn't do it alone – would I help him? Of course I agreed and for the next six months, after school and at week-ends, we worked on digging out the duck-pond. By the Christmas after that, our pond was finished, complete with swimming ducks.

'To this day, I never pass it without thinking of Paddy and our six months together.'

'What happened him?'

'He got a bit weak in the head and couldn't look after himself properly. He went to live with a nephew over on the old road. A bit before your time!' He laughed.

'When did he die?'

'Years and years ago. The nephew inherited the land between our farm and the grazing fields. He eventually went to England so it just lay here all those years – he was always to come back. Then, out of the blue, he sold it to Con Lynch. Lynch knocked down the ruins of the old cottage and built that big house. He did nothing with this field. I always thought, if I thought about it at all, that it was a piece of land that nobody owned.'

We looked at it. A stretch of scrubland cut off from the Lynch estate by a thick thorn hedge, a huge boulder scattered with gorse bushes rising up to one side of the pond.

'Maybe nobody does own it.'

'It's not possible. O'Neill says land has to have an owner. You just have to find him. Or her. It didn't matter until Con Lynch came along.' He looked into the distance. 'I can't blame myself enough. I should have known. What use would this meadow be to anyone, except with the other land? There's no access to it ...Come on, time to go home. The dew is beginning to fall.'

As I lay awake thinking about it all, I couldn't believe that this was happening to us. There had to be a way out.

I fell asleep and dreamed that Piggy and I were chasing the Lynch family into the river. Only I couldn't get him to move fast enough. He was plodding along as slowly as he had done in Athenry show-ring. They were going to get away.

It's great to have parents who share their problems with you. Or is it?

8 The Volunteer

'Ordinarily,' explained Nick, 'it would take three months to get a rider ready for the shows.' He fiddled with his half-full mug of coffee at the kitchen table. 'And here we are with the show season already in full swing.'

Mom, Dad and I were listening intently. It was the day after the Athenry Show and we had all gathered to hear what Nick proposed to do about Piggy and me.

'First,' went on Nick, 'we're got to work on getting Piggy's weight down.'

'Poor Piggy!' Mom, who was always feeding him bits and pieces, was sympathetic. 'He's not really overweight, is he?'

'He's fat,' said Nick firmly. 'And most judges don't like fat ponies. He'll always lose marks for conformation. I reckon he could easily lose sixty pounds. He also needs a lot of exercise and schooling to develop his neck and hind quarters and tighten up his belly.'

I knew I'd be next. What was in store for me?

'Second, I need to help Clare with her riding. She must learn to sit firmly in the saddle so that she won't end up on Piggy's neck every time she goes over a fence. Her seat should be so secure she's never pulled out of the saddle. Also, I have to teach her to give the right signals for canter leads, and we must work on her individual test.'

'Nick?' Mom was looking worried. 'Do you really have the time to spend with Clare and Piggy? It's your holiday.'

'Of course we'll gladly pay you,' said Dad. 'We couldn't let you do it for nothing.'

'Yes, I do have the time, and, No, you will not pay me,' Nick said smiling. 'It's only a small return for all the hours you minded me when I was younger and Uncle John used to park me here when he was going around the country on his calls.'

'Do you think Piggy is good enough to spend time on?' asked Mom.

'Definitely. He has the makings of a first-class hunter pony. He's bold and free over his fences. He's a good mover and a kind and honest type – except for the occasional naughtiness.' Nick looked at me. 'I like him a lot. His shape is right, he has natural balance, and he'll be so much better when he's trimmed down.'

'We'll do everything we can to help,' promised Mom.

'Great! If we're going to get Clare and Piggy going, it will take teamwork. We'll all have to help. I've made a list,' pulling a small pad of paper from his jeans pockets. 'This shows what everyone has to do and gives the daily timetable.'

Mom took it and studied it. 'I'll stick it on the fridge door so everyone will know what they're supposed to be doing at any time.' As she read it

over, a puzzled frown appeared. 'Eight o'clock –
lesson. Nine to eleven – hack for five miles. That's
three hours.'

'Three hours,' I echoed. 'I've never ridden Piggy
for more than an hour a day.'

'And it shows,' said Nick bluntly. 'If you want to
get Piggy into top condition, he'll need exercise. Lots
of it. We'll start off on a light programme, then
gradually increase it as he – and you – get fitter.'

'What sort of programme?' asked Dad.

'A combination of lunge work, ring work and a
long hack.'

We must have all looked blank because Nick
smiled. 'Don't worry – I'll explain as we go along.
Remember, it's very important to vary the exercise so
Piggy won't become bored. No animal likes trotting
around a ring hour after hour, day after day.'

'Week-ends off, I suppose,' said Mom brightly.

'Seven days a week, except for a show day,' said
Nick. 'I know it's going to be tough going – but
there's no other way.'

Mom looked at me. I knew what she was thinking.
I'd be all enthusiasm for a week. Then I'd give up
and opt out.

'I'll do it, Mom,' I said. 'I won't let Nick down. I
promise.'

'When do you start?' asked Dad.

'Right now.'

As soon as Mom had stuck the list up, Dad and I
studied it.

Nick was right; it was going to be tough going.

Daily Schedule				
Time	*Person – Job*	*Pony Nuts*	*Hay*	*Treats*
7 am	Dad – feed	$\frac{3}{4}$ lb		
8 am	Clare– lesson			
9 am	Clare – 5 mile hack			
11 am	Clare – mucking out			Carrot
11 am	Dad – feed		2 lb	
Noon	Clare – groom			
1 pm	Dad – feed	1 lb		
2 pm	Dad – feed		2 lb	
6 pm	Dad – feed	$\frac{3}{4}$ lb		
11 pm	Dad – feed		$3\frac{1}{2}$ lb	
11 pm	Clare			Apple

'I don't seem to have much to do,' said Mom, looking glum.

'You've got to feed the troops,' smiled Dad.

'Starting from now. All this talk about exercise and hard training is making me hungry. You'll have a sandwich, Nick, before you start?'

A block of cheddar cheese, tomatoes, spring onions, frilly lettuce, hard-boiled eggs and bread appeared from the fridge and we all started assembling rough-cut sandwiches.

Half an hour later Nick and I were out in the sand-ring. Mom sat on the rail watching. It was our first lesson. Day one of the rest of my life.

Nick had fixed a long rein to Piggy and was explaining to Mom what he was going to do.

'Back home we used to start each training day with ten or fifteen minutes work on the lunge – that's a lunge rein I've put on him. It's quite simple. I stand in the centre of the ring, holding the lunge line in one hand, the lunge whip in the other, and get Piggy to move around me. Distance from me should be about twenty meters. First, I'll walk Piggy… Clare, catch him by the bridle and get him moving.'

Piggy responded and soon he was walking around in a perfect circle. Then Nick reversed the direction.

'He's doing perfectly. Probably did this before so he knows the routine… Now, we'll get him to trot.'

After trotting in each direction, Piggy was put into a brief canter. Then we joined Mom and Nick.

'The idea behind lungeing,' said Nick, 'apart from

the exercise, is that it helps a pony to develop a smooth even gait. Also, it improves his balance and suppleness. Once I get him warmed up, I'll get Clare to ride him while he's still on the lungeing rein. This will teach her to ride without reins and give her a stronger and more independent seat – no more snatching at his mane! I'll get her to do a lot of exercises while sitting in the saddle, both at the walk and trot... Come on, Clare. Let's give it a go.'

We saddled Piggy and I got up, feeling utterly lost without the reins. Nick was beside me.

'You must ride with more leg contact. Piggy doesn't know what you want him to do. Ask him to move forward by squeezing him with your legs.' He took hold of one of my legs and pushed it against Piggy's side to show me what he meant.

I squeezed – and Piggy moved forward.

'Great! That's the idea. You'll soon learn to control him without using the reins to balance on.'

'How long do you keep her on the lungeing rein?' called Mom.

'We'll work up to half an hour. Then we'll do some riding without it. Piggy is used to an hour or so of riding a day so we can increase that gradually. We'll practise lots of circles and figures-of-eight.'

I was quite happy sitting on Piggy's back, walking around in a circle, legs against his side. I hoped he knew there was a new-style rider on board.

'Now we'll try a sitting trot,' said Nick. 'Relax your body. If you're too rigid, you'll bounce.'

He didn't suggest cantering to my utter relief and

we went back to Mom.

I had a question for Nick. 'This five-mile hack? What is it?'

'It just means exercising a pony without making him do any hard work. He walks some of the time, then trots, either along roads or broken country. It's the best way for getting a pony fit. It will harden his legs, especially if you trot him up any hills and walk down them. I've mapped out some good routes for Clare that will give lots of variety.

'One ends up at the river next to Clarin Bridge. There's a perfect spot next to the bridge where he can stand knee-deep in the water for a five or ten minutes soak. There's no better way to cool off his legs before walking home.'

'Roads?' Mom sounded doubtful. 'Will she be safe?'

'Perfectly. She'll be okay once she's learned the road code. Anyway, I'll be with her on my bike all the time.'

'Take one of our horses if you want to,' said Mom. 'Clare knows where the tack is.'

9 Good News – Bad News

The weather stayed hot and dry, turning the sand-ring into a dust-bowl. Piggy had begun to cough – Dad thought it was because of the dust – so Nick suggested that we practise in one of the grass paddocks. There was a fenced-in area behind the chestnut-tree and Nick spent an afternoon marking out a figure-of-eight pattern for me to follow. He sprinkled a bag of lime (that Dad kept in the shed for white-washing) along the ground. The white powder against the short cropped green grass made an easy track for me to follow.

I felt I was getting better. Piggy seemed to respond to my legs more readily and I didn't have to kick him furiously to get him into a trot or a canter. And when I jumped I was no longer hoisted up on his neck. My individual test was also improving.

One day as we were starting on our umpteenth figure-of-eight, Piggy's body suddenly tensed. He turned his head, his ears cupped forward listening, and his eyes widened. Danger signals! Nick and I turned to see what had frightened him so.

I burst out laughing when I saw what looked like a purple horse-eating monster approaching. It was Maggie, wearing a bright purple flounced sun-dress.

'Hi! Hot enough for the two of ye,' she said, wiping

a freckly arm across her forehead. 'What are ye doin'?'

'My individual test,' I explained. 'I'd better get on with it.'

'Hold on a minute,' said Nick. 'I've had a great idea. Clare, do your test, exactly as if you were at the Loughrea Show... and we'll let Maggie be the judge. She's dressed for the occasion.'

We all laughed, knowing full well that the judges nearly always wore plain-coloured suits and trim matching hats.

'I'll stand by the fence to get a good overall view of you and Piggy. Maggie, you come into the centre of the ring.' Then, as we both giggled, he said sharply, 'Clare, be serious. This time tomorrow you'll be at Loughrea. Just about to start your individual test.'

That soon sobered me up. Loughrea Show was on the next day. It was almost two weeks since we had started serious training and it would be the test of whether Piggy and I were competition material or not.

'Next competitor, please,' Maggie called out in an official tone.

A warm breeze rustled the leaves in the trees beside me and whipped a few loose strands of hair across my face. Piggy and I approached her and I bowed.

'Please walk forward and trot back. Then you may continue your test,' instructed Maggie in a posh voice.

'Yes, Ma'am,' I said and pushed Piggy into a lively

walk. I did my best to keep him straight, eyeing a top stone on the river wall as my line. I turned him after twenty yards and asked him to trot back. The increase in pace made him cough. I had to stop and wait for him to clear his throat.

'Go on, Clare,' yelled Nick. 'You know that part of the test anyway. Now the figure-of-eight.'

I picked up a trot again on my way to the start of my figure-of-eight. I tried not to look at the well-marked track but to sense the size and shape of the two connected circles. I concentrated on keeping Piggy forward but balanced at the same time, while trying to remember everything Nick had taught me.

When we reached the start of the figure I sat deep in my saddle. A nudge behind the girth with my outside leg and a check with my inside rein signalled Piggy for a canter. I looked down at his shoulder to see if he was on the correct lead.

'Clare, don't look down,' shouted Nick. 'You must *feel* which shoulder is ahead.'

Having already seen that I was on the correct lead I kept going and completed the circle. I slowed Piggy back to a trot for three strides and then signalled for the opposite lead. My heart felt as if it had stopped. I feared the worst. I had to look down. His lead was correct!

'Yes!' I shouted triumphantly to myself. 'Good boy!' I kept cantering until I finished the second circle, then I headed for the outside of the ring for the gallop.

'Don't gallop until you get to the long side of the ring,' instructed Nick. 'It's not a free-for-all. You just want to show the judge you can lengthen Piggy's stride and pace. And for goodness sake, pull up in plenty of time.'

'How was that?' I asked breathlessly after finishing my test, coming to a halt in front of Maggie.

'Miss Fox, you're supposed to salute and not talk to the judge,' Maggie kidded. 'I'll have to deduct three points.'

Piggy coughed again and tried to get his head down in order to snatch a bite of grass.

'Not again… this coughing is beginning to get to me,' I complained.

'Don't worry,' reassured Nick 'It's probably just the dust. I'll tell your dad to dampen Piggy's hay from now on before giving it to him... Now for more important matters. That, Clare, is what I call a dramatic improvement. What do you think, Most Honourable Judge?'

Maggie pretended to look at a score-sheet. She turned towards me. 'I'm giving you top marks: twenty points for manner and performance, twenty marks for conformation, movement and type.' Then she threw her arms into the air. 'Hurrah! Timber Twig is the Champion of Champions!'

'Great!' I thought. 'My legs are killing me from all the squeezing and nudging to get Piggy moving. And I still have my five-mile hack to do. Will I ever live to see Loughrea tomorrow?'

When I got back from the hack and put Piggy in his stable I collapsed into the well-worn armchair in the corner of the kitchen. Tiny jumped on top of me.

'I need a bath but I'm too tired,' I told Mom who was sitting at the table studying a list. 'What on earth are you doing?'

'I'm making a check-list,' she said. 'I've decided to copy Nick's methods and get it all down on paper.'

'What's "all"?'

'Show check-list. In future, instead of us all tearing around on the morning of a show looking for missing items and forgetting bits and pieces, it's all going to be put down. In writing.' She handed me a sheet of paper.

Horse Show Check-List

Dad: Check Piggy's shoes.
Diesel in jeep.
Check tyres and lights on jeep and horse-box.
Put in 5-gallon container of water, plus bucket.
Put in net of hay.

Mom: Entries to show, plus Piggy's passport.
First-aid kit. Sun screen.
Clean and oil tack – saddle, girth, leathers, bridle.
Picnic lunch
Wash Piggy. Plait mane. Bandage tail.
Check riding clothes – riding-coat, jodhpurs plus clips, jodhpur boots, tie and tie-pin, riding-shirt, riding-hat, riding-whip, gloves, raincoats.

Nick: Pack grooming kit for show, including hoof-oil and brush.
Ready Piggy for travelling – head-collar, lead, rug.

Clare: Groom Piggy.
Muck out stable.

'That's great, Mom. You've got it all here,' I said handing it back to her, putting off the moment when I would have to pull myself out of the chair and crawl upstairs for a bath. One thing though; I noticed that I wasn't as sore as I used to be when we first started training, when I was a mass of aching muscles after every lesson.

Just then Dad walked in.

'You're back early,' said Mom, getting up to put on the kettle. 'I thought you were going over to John's to collect some medicine.'

'I didn't.' He sat down and looked at both of us. 'That phone call this morning was from O'Neill. He wanted to see me. Nothing urgent, he said. But I thought the sooner I saw him the better.'

'What happened?' asked Mom.

'I know,' I said, getting up excitedly. 'He found something!' I remembered that he was to look up deeds or something.

'No,' said Dad in a dispirited way. 'He found nothing. Absolutely nothing.'

'What does that mean?'

'It seems we bought the grazing fields all right but there's no mention whatsoever of a right of way to get to them. It's all there in black and white. Con Lynch owns the land beside us, from the road to the river. And he says we can't cross his land.'

I felt a vague fluttering in my stomach. 'But I thought you said we has a right of... whatever it was.'

'A right of way. So we have – on the grounds that we've always used that field to move the cattle across.'

'Then what's the problem?' Mom sounded impatient. 'What does O'Neill say?'

Dad shrugged his shoulders. 'He says it's a grey

area. There seem to be no certainties when it comes to rights of way. It's not an ordinary public right of way, you see. It's used only by us. And Con Lynch has title to that land.'

'A grey area?' Mom looked incredulous. 'You go to a solicitor to get advice. He should be telling you what to do. Not waffling away about grey areas.'

'Well, he has given me some advice.'

'And what's that?'

'He thinks I should make Con Lynch an offer for the field. Thinks he doesn't really want it for himself. He's just being awkward.'

Mom still had that incredulous look. 'He wants us to buy something to give us a right of way – that we already have.'

'It may not be so easy to prove we have it.'

'Then why don't we take it to court and find out?'

'It would cost a lot of money. And if we lost the case – and O'Neill says it's not an open and shut one – we would have to pay all our expenses. And Con Lynch's as well. Apart from all that, it would be two or three years before the case was heard. And we'd be living in uncertainty all that time… O'Neill says it would be far better to try and settle it out of court. It would save us a lot of hassle.'

'And what's all this going to cost?'

'Depends. It's only about four acres. But the value will depend on whether it's rated agricultural land or not. And it's on a river.'

Mom got up. 'Time I started getting the dinner.'

'What do you think I should do about the field?'

'I'll leave it to you two "experts".' There was a heavy emphasis on the word and Dad winced. She smiled at him. 'Go on and buy it. We'll find the money somewhere.'

Dad wandered off and I began to lay the table.

'Mom, will it be all right?'

'Of course it will. What use would that little bit of rough land be to Con Lynch. He'd have to take it apart. Blast that rock away and fill in the pond. He'll probably reckon a bit of cash in hand is better – I hear he's greedy for money. Anyway, I'm sure he wants to live in peace with his neighbours.'

Mom was almost as bad as Maggie at seeing silver linings.

'But where will we get the money?'

'We'll find it. The banks are awash with it at the moment...hey, weren't you going to have a hot bath?'

10 Loughrea

'I don't see a problem with any of the fences,' Nick said to me as we left the ring after walking the course at Loughrea Show.

We had come over with the O'Connors – Mr O'Connor was showing his famous bullock. Maggie had come along but opted out of competing – too hot, she said, for anything but eating ice-cream. Mom and Dad had stayed away. Nick suggested to them that it would be better if I stood on my own two feet. For a change.

'But I still don't see why they won't let me show Piggy the fences,' I grumbled. 'He'll never jump them for me.'

'Clare, I told you before that this is classified as an *Open* Working Hunter Class – where you *can't* show the pony the fences beforehand. You usually ride in the Novice Working Hunter Class, where you can. Today they're only offering the Open Class. But you'll be fine. You saw the fences and that's all that matters. They're just plain poles and a bit of brush. Now, pull yourself together.'

I had to admit that although it was a blow not to be able to walk the course mounted on Piggy I never felt more confident. Just having Nick beside me gave me courage. He was so good at explaining how to ride each fence, where to turn, and when to change canter leads. He was always so positive. I guess some of his drive just had to brush off on me. Mom had always done her best but she didn't have the experience Nick had.

'Let's get warmed up and we'll see how many others are in your class,' suggested Nick. 'I think you should jump third or fourth. That'll give you enough time to see if there are any tricky fences or turns but not enough time to lose your nerve. Now, go and tell the ring steward when you want to jump and I'll go and get Piggy. See you in the warm-up ring.'

The ring steward had his sign-up sheet in hand. I could see there were several names on it already. 'I have only the first, third or tenth spot still open.'

'Third, please,' I said, thinking it had been a close shave. Nick had told me to go to the ring steward when we arrived but I had persuaded him to walk the course first. 'My name is…'

I was interrupted by a sudden shove. Standing behind me was Brenda Fahy, snapping her wad of chewing-gum. She brushed by me.

'I was told by the show director, Mr Ryan, that Kelly Lynch is to jump third. Kelly Lynch on Moonstepper. Her show number is twelve. I've to go back and confirm this with him.'

'Well, of course, if Mr Ryan says so, I'll put her down.' He turned to me. Seeing my face, his cracked into a smile. 'You don't mind jumping first, do you? You'll set the standard! Now, name and number.'

I was so shocked at what had just happened that I couldn't speak. Satisfied that I wasn't going to complain, Brenda smirked at me before turning and disappearing into the crowd.

'I don't believe she had the cheek,' fumed Nick when I joined him in the warm-up ring. 'If only I'd been there, I'd have refused to budge. You should have called for Mr Ryan. It was a try-on. However, it's over and done with now. And the steward was right – you've a chance to set the standard.'

'Will the first rider, Clare Fox riding Timber Twig, please enter the ring.'

Nick gave me a pat on the leg and said, 'Forget Kelly and Brenda. Just concentrate on the course, keep an even canter and ride at your fences like you mean it. Good luck and smile. You can do it... remember you always jump first at home.'

He was right. On our practice courses at home I was well used to jumping without someone going first. Oddly, the confrontation with Brenda hadn't really upset me, just strengthened my determination. I was getting fitter in more ways than one.

Piggy jumped the eight fences easily and I felt much more in control of him than ever before. Nick had taught me how to 'see a stride', giving Piggy the right signal at the right time to take off for a fence. I was now able to stay balanced in the saddle and let my hands move independently of my seat.

I knew by Nick's smile when I left the ring that I had done well.

Because the course was easy, there were seven clear rounds including mine – and Kelly's. She was called back second; I was called third.

I couldn't believe it when I heard my number being called in third place. But before I could say a word, Nick was saying quietly but firmly, 'Don't blow it. Get yourself together. I mean it. If you don't, you'll throw away your chance of keeping third place. Listen to the judge and watch how the first two ride their test. Good luck.' He gave Piggy a gentle slap on the rump as I rode back to the ring.

After the trot and the canter in both directions, the judge asked us to line up according to number. As I rode in beside Kelly she looked at me dismissively; I kept my eyes straight ahead. I watched carefully as the first rider and Kelly rode their figures-of-eight. I noted where they started their gallop and where they slowed back to a canter and then a trot. I watched how they both bowed. I watched every little thing.

I don't remember a thing about my own test – except that it happened and I got through it. I now awaited the final decision.

I was still in a half trance when I felt Nick's hand on my arm.

'Clare, quick! Get down. We've got to strip Piggy.'

'What?'

'Hurry! Get down and I'll explain later,' hardly giving me time to dismount before he had Piggy's girth undone and saddle off and on the ground behind us.

'What's happening?' I asked, bewildered. I noticed that all six riders were also on the ground, saddles off, helpers brushing over their ponies. Brenda was hard at work on Moonstepper.

'It's called stripping. I didn't think you'd have to do it. Most judges don't bother with it at small shows.' Nick was rubbing Piggy's glowing coat with a cloth. 'I'll explain it all later. But watch what the first two riders are doing. You've got to do the same.'

I watched the first rider walk from the line with his pony and halt before the judge. After she looked at the pony carefully from all sides, she asked the rider to walk the pony away from her in a straight line and trot back, just as we did when we were mounted.

Now it was our turn. I was suddenly thankful that we had done all that hard work on Piggy. He really looked trim and fit. Nick confirmed it. 'Piggy looks super,' he whispered as he helped me to resaddle him. Then we had to do a final walk around the ring.

Very shortly afterwards, the loudspeaker blared: 'First prize goes to Kelly Lynch riding Moonstepper. Second prize to David Lawson riding Storm. And third prize to Clare Fox riding Timber Twig.'

'I've done it!' I whispered again and again as we did our victory gallop before leaving the ring.

'Fan...tas...tic!' yelled Maggie rushing up. 'Come on, the ice-cream's on me.'

'Make mine a double with raspberry topping,' said Nick.

'Ye'll be lucky!' kidded Maggie, giving him a punch that nearly knocked him into Piggy. 'Wait till ye hear what I'm goin' to have on your round.'

'Thanks for taking us all to the show, Mr O'Connor,' I said appreciatively, standing beside the battered lorry's cab window. 'You're the best.'

'Me, too. Thanks for the lift. We all had a great day. Sorry the bullock didn't score,' added Nick. 'See you, Mags. Make sure you give that lazy race-horse of yours a treat. He deserves it – for letting us win a prize.'

'You...' began Maggie but Mr O'Connor was already driving away.

Nick and I waved, my other hand clutching my yellow rosette. I could feel my shirt sticking to me. My arms were a mixture of red and grey, sunburn mixed with grime. I could feel a burning sting on my nose and forehead. I knew I'd be as red as a beet in the morning. Why couldn't I turn an enviable bronzy colour instead? And it was all my own fault: I'd forgotten the sun screen.

'Third place! Who would ever think you'd pull that off after less than a fortnight's work,' Nick joked. 'That coach of yours needs a medal!... Here, give me Piggy and I'll look after him. You go in and tell the folks the good news.'

'Hi, Mom, we're back,' I shouted when I reached the kitchen door. I couldn't help the lilt in my voice. 'Guess what?'

'Tell me quick, I hate suspense,' said Mom. 'I'm sure you did just great.' Mom always said that, even if she suspected I hadn't. Dad appeared from the sitting-room, Rex at his heels.

'I came third! Piggy and I came third! Dad, did you hear? Look, here's the rosette. Nick is the best. We did it! We did it!'

'Never doubted it for a moment,' chuckled Dad. 'Next time it'll be the red.'

'Where's Nick? I have a nice cheese pizza for the pair of you. And tossed salad. I'm sure you had nothing decent to eat all day.'

As Nick and I were devouring our supper Mom sat with us, listening while we recounted the events of the day. When Dad came back after checking the cows and calves we were still at it.

'Give over,' he said. 'I feel as if I'm jumping the course myself... Now, let's see that rosette of yours again.'

I went into the sitting-room where I retrieved it from the lampshade I'd hung it on. He and I studied it in detail under the kitchen light.

Nick left shortly afterwards. At the door he turned. 'See you in the morning. Eight o'clock sharp.'

'Can't she have one morning in bed?' pleaded Mom.

'Not a chance. Not if she wants a red rosette or two.'

'Well, she'll sleep like a log,' said Dad.

Easier said than done. In bed, I kept reliving every moment of that jumping round. Fence by fence. Not to mention my almost perfect figure-of-eight.

11 Three Letters

'Clare, there's a letter for you,' Mom's voice called up the back stairs. Maggie and I were deeply engrossed in making stable rugs for our joint miniature horse collection.

'Who's the lucky lad?' Maggie teased, sitting cross-legged on my bedroom floor, surrounded by pieces of fabric.

'I'll be back in a sec,' I said, leaping up and making a dash for the stairs. 'Don't cut any more squares until I get back. Promise?' I yelled behind me.

'Who's it from?' I shouted as I ran down into the kitchen.

'How would I know?' Mom answered, fingering two other letters on the kitchen table. 'Open it and see.'

'Mom! Read this... it can't be true,' I whispered, handing her a short typewritten sheet. She took it from me, pulled out a chair, sat down and began to read. I listened, my heart racing:

BALLINASLOE SHOW SOCIETY
is pleased to inform that
CLARE FOX
and his/her pony
TIMBER TWIG

have qualified to ride in the
ALL-IRELAND WORKING HUNTER PONY
CHAMPIONSHIP,
to be held on September 1st in the showgrounds.
If you wish to compete, please notify the
SHOW SECRETARY at 0905 22244

Mom handed the letter back to me. 'Apparently you qualified by coming third at Loughrea.'

'Mom, can I go? Oh, please can I go?' I begged, jumping up and dancing around the kitchen table. 'Wait until I tell Maggie... and I must see Nick.'

'Wait a minute, Clare. Before you go, look at this.' She showed me another envelope, just the same as mine. Same size. Same neat typewritten address label. Same postmark.

'It's addressed to Kelly Lynch. How did we get it?'

'The postman delivered it here by mistake.'

'What are you going to do with it?'

'I think you and Maggie should walk down and give the letter to her. It's probably also about Ball-inasloe.'

'I don't know, Mom. Why can't we take it back to the post office?'

'And pass by Lynchs on the way? That's a bit ridiculous. If it's about Ballinasloe she must be waiting for it.'

'Kelly Lynch? She *knows* she's qualified.'

Mom handed me the letter. 'Now, don't be so difficult. It's a glorious day. You girls can go across the fields and be there in five minutes. No buts.'

'Okay, but I'd rather not,' I grumbled, heading slowly towards the back stairs to tell Maggie the news. About Ballinasloe. And having to play postman.

'Maggie, you ring the bell,' I suggested as we approached the Lynch house. We had cut across our fields in no time but thought it best to go around to the front of the house. No one ever used the back door to a mansion – at least not in any of the TV programmes we'd ever seen.

'I'll ring but what if there's a bloomin' attack dog.' Maggie was losing her nerve. 'I wish we'd brought Rex and Tiny.'

'It won't bite you. Not unless it's a Rottweiler and I don't think the Lynchs have one. Go on and ring.'

She pushed the door-bell and we both stood back, ready to take to our heels if a Rottweiler appeared. It didn't. The door was opened by a small middle-aged woman dressed in a white blouse and black skirt.

'Can I help you?' she asked pleasantly.

'Um... you see... I have this letter that's not mine,' I mumbled. 'The postman gave it to us. And it's not for us. It's for Kelly. Will you give it to her?'

'Kelly is in the conservatory. Why don't you give it to her yourselves?' she asked. 'Please follow me.'

Before I had a chance to refuse, she turned and went into the house, leaving the door open. Maggie rolled her eyes, shrugged her shoulders and followed. So did I, still holding the letter. I shut the door behind me.

Walking into the Lynch house was like walking into a dream world, the kind you see in programmes on 'Great Houses' on TV. There was a circular hall and through open doors I could see into most of the rooms. I got a general impression of strong rich colours, matching curtains and chairs, lots of antique-looking furniture, paintings in gilded frames, crystal bowls and silver ornaments.

'I'm Vera Lane, the Lynchs' housekeeper. I think you girls are from the farm down the road. Am I right?' the small woman said as we followed her through the hall to a door at the far end. She opened it.

'Here we are. Kelly, you have two visitors.'

A huge sun-room looked out on to a terrace with steps down to a velvet lawn. A fountain bubbled in the centre. Kelly was sitting on an overstuffed sofa that almost dwarfed her, a top-of-the-pops magazine in her lap, She was listening to a tape on her Discman. She said nothing as we approached her, didn't even remove her headphone.

'Hi, Kelly. Mags and I just came over to give you this letter.' I handed it to her. 'I got one like it today. It's about Ballinasloe.'

Kelly still said nothing. She opened the letter, threw it aside carelessly. 'Oh, that, I was expecting it. Of course I knew I'd qualified.'

'In that case, I'm sorry we bothered you.' I turned to go. I was furious with Mom. Would she never understand about people like Kelly?

'No, hold on,' said Kelly, springing to her feet.

'Thanks for bringing it over. Do you want to sit down for a moment? Have a Coke?'

'No,' I said shortly.

'We have to go back and baby-sit,' explained Maggie, trying to soften my rudeness. It wasn't entirely true.

I turned at the door. Kelly had resumed her seat and switched on her Discman again. She didn't say anything to us. The silence was deafening. Where was Mrs Lynch? Mr Lynch? Was there nobody there other than the nice housekeeper? The house was beautiful but so cold and lonely.

'Good luck,' I said, feeling I'd been a bit churlish. She didn't reply. Maggie and I went back across the hall and let ourselves out through the front door as quietly as possible

'I could have done with an iced Coke,' said Maggie as we went over the fields.

I gave her a withering look.

'Did you give Kelly Lynch her letter?' Mom asked when we got back. 'Their house must be beautiful.'

'Yes, Mom,' I replied. 'She's in the Championship too. And, yes, the house is beautiful.'

'Do they have an indoor swimming pool?' asked Sam.

'How should I know?' I answered. 'We didn't get a guided tour.'

'Did you see Mr Lynch?' asked Dad.

'No, we didn't see anyone except Kelly and a nice housekeeper... Why do you ask?'

'Just checking,' Dad said. He sounded exasperated. 'O'Neill had this letter from his solicitor saying he was away in the States on business and wouldn't be back for a few weeks.'

'So we won't know about buying the field for *another* few weeks.' Mom sound equally exasperated. To change the subject, she asked, 'How's Piggy today?'

Piggy still had that nagging cough that had begun about the time we started serious training. Short, sharp coughs, followed by a lot of snorting. It was as if he was trying to clear something out of his throat. If it was just a case of dust the move to the grass paddock should have cleared it. But it hadn't. It had become deeper-sounding and more debilitating.

Now if he had an attack when I was riding him, he would have to come to a complete stop, drop his head and brace himself for the coughing fit. Nick and I were beginning to wonder if it was something more serious than dust.

I had taken Piggy to three other shows since the one in Loughrea. We had managed to get placed fourth, second, and third. So I was really looking forward to riding in the Scariff Show this week-end. I was certain I could at least get a third place again. And now this! I knew from the vet columns in my pony magazines that a virus cough could take months to get rid of. Just my luck, with the Championship coming up and everything going so well. For me that was. Not for Piggy. I didn't want to think about it. I hated to see him sick.

Mom was looking at me. I hadn't answered her. She knew I'd gone to check on him before Maggie and I went over to the Lynchs.

'I think he's better,' I lied.

12 Heartbreak

But Piggy wasn't better. Next morning at breakfast we could hear him coughing in his stable. It went on and on and on.

'We'll have to get John in to check him,' said Dad, concerned. 'There's something wrong with that pony.'

'Not a virus, I hope.' Dad and I were in the stable watching John examining Piggy.

'I wouldn't think so,' holding the thermometer up to catch the light. 'He has no temperature and his glands seem normal. But you never know what he could have picked up from another pony – you'll find every known infection walking around a show.'

'Can you give him anything for it?' Dad was anxiously shuffling a bit of bedding with his foot.

'I'll start him on an antibiotic, just to be on the safe side. I'll leave the bottle and you can inject him yourself for the next four days.'

'What about exercise?' queried Dad. 'Will it do him any harm?'

'I'd lay him off work for the next few days. No point risking his wind.'

'But what about Scariff on Saturday?' I had to interrupt. 'Piggy has to be all right. We've got to go. I've paid for my class and everything. Oh, please.'

'I'm afraid you'll have to give the show a miss. Piggy's health is more important than any show.'

I gulped. It was suddenly looking serious. Paying for my entry was my way of pretending he was going to be better. It hadn't worked.

'Now, we'll leave him in peace. Clare, make sure you have his door well latched. You know he's a divil for escaping.'

As I left he gave a long, low, choking cough. I could feel it tear at my own lungs. I only wished I was the one suffering.

The three of us sat on the stone wall above the river-bank, tossing pebbles into the shrunken bed below. The stretch of fine weather had dried the river to a small stagnant stream. Maggie and I were dressed in light cotton shirts and shorts. Nick, ignoring the sweltering heat, wore denim jeans and a polo shirt.

The afternoon sun was at its hottest. Nothing stirred except the noisy black crows flitting in and out of the ripening barley fields beyond. Rex and Tiny lay at the base of the wall, alternating between panting and snapping at the midges that swarmed around them.

'A rest won't do Piggy any harm,' Maggie was saying. 'I've decided to give Rambo a break as well. What do ye think?'

'It certainly won't do *him* any harm,' replied Nick. 'Might even improve his mood to get away from you for a day or two.' He gave her a playful punch in the arm.

'Brat!' Maggie responded and quickly punched him back. We all laughed. It felt good and the black mood caused by Piggy's illness lifted for a few minutes. He had now been on antibiotics for three days. We all tried to tell ourselves he was improving.

'I think we should go to Scariff tomorrow anyway,' proposed Nick. 'You can learn a lot watching other people ride, especially from the mistakes they make. Are you on, Clare?'

'I don't know, I don't feel up to much. I might stay home and help Mom in the garden,' I said weakly.

'That's a load of rubbish, 'snapped Maggie. 'Get off it. Ye're coming with us and that's that. Dad has the bullock goin'. He'll bring us. We can take a picnic and everything.'

'Sounds good. Uncle John's off tomorrow so I'll be free,' put in Nick. 'As long as we can get Weeping Heart here to agree.'

'Ha!' I said haughtily. 'I'll race you two to the rope swing. We'll see who's the real Weeping Heart.'

The three of us whooped and shouted and tore off like lunatics towards the chestnut-tree, Rex and Tiny barking and yapping at our heels. For the moment we forgot the dead heat of the summer and the darker gloom of Piggy's poor health.

'Sam, where's Dad?' I crossed the yard to where he was tinkering with the chain on his bike.

Sam had make it quite clear to Mom and Dad that he had no interest in the farm. He wanted to be a mechanic and work on racing-cars. His bicycle was the closest thing to a Ferrari that he had so he spent hours taking it apart and then rebuilding it again.

'Dunno,' Sam mumbled, not even bothering to look up. He continued to fiddle with the chain.

'Sam, Mom is going to kill you. You've got grease all over your clothes,' I warned, stepping over all the dismantled greasy bits and bolts scattered on the ground.

'So?' Sam kept on working. 'I need to get this fixed in case Colm comes over. We might be going camping.'

I heard Dad's tractor coming up the farmyard road. It had a distinct whirring sound that no other tractor made. And when it was a few yards away, just like clockwork, it made a certain slowing-up sound as Dad took his foot off the accelerator to make the turn into the yard. Rex and Tiny appeared from nowhere with tails wagging.

'Hi, Daddy,' I called as he climbed down from the tractor.

'How's my best girl?' he asked, giving my hair a gentle tweak. 'I see your brother is up to no good. Sam Fox, I'll hang you upside down if I find any of my tools missing.'

Sam gave him a disgusted look.

'Dad, is it all right for me to go to Scariff Show tomorrow? Mr O'Connor has the bullock entered so he can give us a lift. Nick is going as well.'

'Sounds good but check with your Mom. Where is she? I'm half-starved with the thirst and hunger.' He headed towards the back door with me close behind.

I didn't ask him whether there was any news from
O'Neill. But he seemed happier these days. Making
up his mind to buy the field had obviously taken a
weight off his mind.

After supper Dad got to his feet. 'Who's coming on
the milk run?'

Since the Lynch letter he had always referred to
going over to check on the cattle as the 'milk run'.

'Not me,' said Mom. 'Have to finish this travel
article, "Europe on 50p a day". Anyone on?'

'Make them an offer,' joked Dad. 'Offer them 25p
a day... Come on, Clare.'

As we went across the duck-pond meadow we played an elaborate cops and robbers routine, skirting the thorn hedge bordering the Lynch land and dropping to hands and knees as we crawled past an exposed bit where there was a gap in the bushes.

'What'll I do if I see any Lynchs?' I whispered.

'Don't fire until you see the whites of their eyes.'

'And if I do see the whites of their eyes?'

'String 'em up... Lynch Law. Very fitting in Galway.'

Getting to our feet, we walked down towards the gate into the grazing fields.

'I don't know how the grass is bearing up.' Dad had a worried look on his face. 'If this weather keeps on much longer, we'll have to start feeding the cattle. There won't be enough grass. It simply isn't growing... Hey, what's that?'

Something bright blue on the gate caught our eyes.

'A plastic bag,' said Dad. 'No wonder people complain about the littered countryside. Though I don't now how it got here from the road.'

But the blue 'bag' wasn't a bag at all. It was one of those big plastic-covered chains that one wound around a gate post and locked.

We were locked out of the grazing fields.

When we came home, Dad told Mom briefly what had happened and rushed in to phone O'Neill.

'I can just picture it,' said Mom as we sat together in the kitchen. 'Probably having a glass of dry sherry before grilled salmon from the river. Wild. Caught today. With béarnaise sauce and chilled white wine. He's not going to be happy about a dope of a farmer ringing him after hours.'

Dad came back and sat down.

'Well,' said Mom. 'What did O'Neill say?'

'He says Lynch is very smart. He could have got an injunction to stop us crossing the duck-pond meadow. But he didn't. Now, by locking the gate into the grazing fields, he's putting it up to *us* to take out an injunction to force him to open the gate.'

'In a word, we have to start the ball rolling?'

'Yes.'

'And pay the bills. I thought O'Neill said it would be costly.'

'So it will.'

'And meanwhile the cattle are left stranded in the grazing fields. Starving to death. I never heard of anything so ridiculous in my life.'

'Oh, we could get them back – on the undertaking that we don't use the duck-pond meadow again. Until after the court case, that is. If we win, that is.'

'Any other crumbs of comfort from O'Neill?'

'He says not to worry. Locking the gate was probably something Lynch had arranged to do before he got our offer to buy – remember he's been away for the past fortnight.'

'I'll cling to that,' said Mom. Her eyes fell on me. 'Clare, are you still up? Off!'

As I went up the back stairs, I could hear the discussion continue.

'One thing,' said Mom. 'Why did he lock the gate

into the grazing fields instead of the one from our farm into the duck-pond meadow?'

'That gate is ours. When my dad bought the grazing fields he made an opening and put in that gateway with stone pillars so that the cows could get into the duck-pond meadow. The other gate was there at the time. It was part of the Gallagher land ...O'Neill says it was a smart move. Not to interfere with our property.'

'Why,' said Mom – I could hear her getting to her feet – 'do I have this feeling that O'Neill secretly admires the man? Is it part of the way we are to admire fixers and chancers? Talk about the playboy of the western world!'

I passed Sam's bedroom. He was pitting his wits against Vadar or Vartar or something equally out of this world. Maybe if Dad and Mom had been into electronic games at Sam's age, they would have been able to make mincemeat of Lynch. And O'Neill.

It was only a thought. On balance, I was glad I was going to Scariff Show tomorrow.

13 Scariff

'Whoa, boy, Steady now. Easy now.' As we went through the car park eating curried chips, a girl's voice came to our ears through the horse-boxes and lorries. Someone was trying to load a horse.

We had had a great day strolling around the showgrounds. First we watched the judging of the young horse classes, taking bets on which entry would win Champion Young Horse of the show. Then we found an empty bench in time to see the lead-rein class. It's always the most glamorous class of the day – men in summer suits and hats leading beribboned children on glossy ponies. Maggie and I adore small ponies, especially when they're plaited to the nines and decorated with ribbons, roses and carnations.

'Takes us back to our youth, doesn't it,' sighed Maggie.

After lunch we decided to watch all the Working Hunter Pony classes. I thought I'd be terribly depressed, observing a class I should have been riding in, but I wasn't. It was actually a relief to be sidelined. No pressure. No nerves. No feeling I must ride well.

Kelly Lynch won our class easily. Moonstepper jumped like a buck and moved like a ballet dancer. I bore Kelly no ill-will; she won the class fair and square. I made a mental note of a few things she did that I planned to try out with Piggy as soon as he was well enough to ride again.

After the 133 class we thought we'd go and see how Mr O'Connor and bullock were doing. That was when we heard the voice in the car park.

'Stop it! Stop messing! What's wrong with you? We're going home. You should be happy. Come on. We'll try it again. In you go. *Please*, Moonstepper, *please*.' It was Kelly Lynch! Beginning to sound desperate. We looked at each other.

Nick was the first to react. 'Come on, let's see if we can help.'

We walked quickly around the row of cars and horse-boxes. Kelly Lynch, face red and beaded with perspiration, was trying to coax Moonstepper into the horse-box. He was visibly upset; his eyes rolled, showing the whites, his coat ran with sweat.

'Do you need a hand?' Nick volunteered. 'He's probably just a bit upset with all the commotion. Kelly, you lead him in and we'll guide from behind.'

She didn't argue. It was tricky operation, but with Kelly leading and Nick gently urging him from behind and Mags and I making soothing noises from both sides of the ramp, we got him in.

'Great job,' said a relieved Nick, latching the back ramp of the horse-box. 'How did he get himself into such a state? Over what?' As there was no reply from Kelly, he went on, 'Are you all right?' She still said nothing, just nodded. She was probably too drained to say anything. We all stood there silently.

'Thanks for helping me,' she said at last. 'He's usually so easy to load... and Joe is always here to help me. I don't know what got into him.'

She still sounded flustered. But as we turned away she said, 'Would you like a Coke? I have cold drinks and some things in the car,' gesturing towards the Mercedes.

'I'll leave you girls to chat,' said Nick. 'I must see the final judging of the bullock class. Who knows? Maybe we'll have a silver cup going home with us. See you in a bit.' He headed off through the parking area to the showgrounds.

I was about to say something when Maggie nudged me and hissed, 'Say yes.'

'Congratulations on your win,' I said. 'You were the best in the class by far.'

'I'll spread out the lot on this car rug,' Kelly said, unfolding a red plaid designer creation with someone's name scrawled across one corner. I noticed it because it was right at my feet.

'Sit down and help yourselves,' she said, opening up a wicker picnic basket. 'How come you weren't riding today?'

'Clare's pony is very bad with the cough,' explained Maggie. 'And I decided to give me guy a break as well. Isn't the heat killin'?'

'Some things,' Kelly had said. Some things! Maggie and I were too gobsmacked to do anything but stare as she set out a bowl filled with jumbo prawns, another with fresh fruit salad – green and purple grapes, peaches, pears and apples – and a

long stick of bread. There were small triangular-cut
sandwiches with the crusts taken off, salted nuts, and
a cooler filled with ice-cold bottles of Coke and
orange.

Maggie and I sank to our knees, kicked off our
runners and dug in as she put down the last item of
the feast – a rich chocolate cake iced in lighter
chocolate swirls.

When we'd stuffed ourselves with that delicious
picnic and were lying back basking in the late
afternoon sun, I couldn't help asking, 'Where are
your Mom and Dad?'

I hadn't meant to sound nosy. It just sort of
slipped out.

'Away as per usual. I think Dad was in Germany
or Switzerland on business – he exports shellfish to a
lot of places. And Mom was off at one of those
health farms in the south of France. They're due
back today. They'll fly over by helicopter from
Dublin.'

'Who brought you to the show?' asked Maggie.

'The missing Joe Larkin, the man who looks after
our garden. He's nice but not interested in horses.
He's gone off with a few of his friends to watch the
tug-of-war. I'm sure he's in the refreshment tent.'

'Where did you get the picnic?' Maggie asked
curiously.

'From Dad's restaurant – it's a seafood restaurant.
They send us out anything we order. The cake is
their speciality. Vera phoned them last night.'

'And how well she packed everything,' I thought,

reflecting on all the little extras like napkins, paper towels and cocktail sticks. Not to mention sun screen.

'Vera's really like my mother,' went on Kelly. 'Probably better. She's here all the time. You met her at the house the other day.'

'Yeh, she's really nice,' I said, remembering the small friendly woman who had asked us in.

'But don't you get a bit lonely without your parents?' asked Maggie. 'I mean being away and stuff.'

'Not really. You get used to it. Dad's business takes him away a lot and Mom often goes with him. She's always shopping – she brings me back a lot of nice things. But I'm not lonely.' She sounded a bit defensive. 'I ride a lot and Brenda comes over to play tennis. And we might go to dinner at Dad's restaurant or the cinema. And I often go to Dublin to stay with my aunt... Sometimes I think Dad and Mom don't know what to do with me. They're always talking of sending me to a boarding-school. I don't know if I want to go or not.'

'Kelly!' A voice came to us across the field. 'You're supposed to have been home by five. And now it's nearly six!'

'Cripes,' whispered Maggie. 'It's the gorilla!'

I looked up and saw a short, thick-set, powerful man. It was Con Lynch. I'd never really seen him at close quarters but Maggie sure had him taped. He would have made a very good gorilla. He ignored us as we scrambled to our feet and concentrated on

Kelly, tapping a gold watch that glinted in the sun.

'Have you forgotten? We're due at the Murphys at six. And you've got to get home and change. Come on.'

Kelly got up slowly. 'Dad, I don't think you've met my friends. Clare Fox and Maggie O'Connor. They're from my school,' she added.

'That crappy little school. High time you were taken away from it. Mixing with...' He looked more closely at me. 'You're one of those Foxes from the farm next door who are giving me such a hard time.'

I stared at him. 'Yes, I'm one of the Foxes. And you're giving *us* a hard time. We've been living there for...'

My voice trailed off. I couldn't believe I had had the courage to speak to him like that.

'That's as may be. Just don't tangle with me... Come on, Kelly.'

'Dad,' drawled Kelly. 'If you gave a hand instead of standing there shouting, the sooner we'd get the stuff packed away.'

Maggie and I started putting things into the handsome wicker case. Mr Lynch actually gave us a hand; he strapped up the basket and folded the rug. Kelly didn't lift a finger.

'Where's Joe?' he shouted.

'At the tug-of-war. I told him to meet me here... later.'

I admired the way she didn't tell on him.

'Well, you can't wait. You'll have to come with me in the jeep. Jaysus, what a mess.' He turned to us. 'Tell Joe to follow on with the horse-box.'

'*Please*,' said Kelly.

'Please,' said Con Lynch.

'That's quite all right,' said Maggie with dignity. 'We always like to help out in an emergency. Especially our friends.'

He turned and ploughed off. Kelly pulled a face at us and followed him. We stared after them.

'Well!' said Maggie. 'Did ye ever? Did ye hear him swearin'?'

'Who are the Murphys?' I asked. Maggie knew everything about everybody in the area.

'They've taken that old castle on the Oranmore road for the summer. Very up in the world. Loaded.

And you know what... they're just another bunch of gorillas.'

As soon as I got home, I rushed out to see Piggy. Did he seem a bit better? I couldn't decide. He didn't cough when I was there. Maybe there was an improvement. But when I went into the house, Mom told me she'd heard him coughing on and off all afternoon.

Over supper I told Dad and Mom about meeting Mr Lynch.

'Maybe he's not as bad as we think he is,' said Mom.

'He's worse,' I said darkly. 'You should have heard him.'

'Maybe if you went to see him,' went on Mom, ignoring me.

'I don't think there's any point, is there?' Dad sounded gloomy. 'O'Neill says not to get involved personally and I'm inclined to agree. Anyway, the ball is in his court. He'll have to reply to that letter.'

14 Dr Joyce

The phone rang. I hoped it wasn't O'Neill with more bad news. Mom quickly went out to answer it. I could hear her voice. I was in the sitting-room watching *The Black Stallion*.

'Ollie! What a surprise! Yes, we're all fine. How are your brood?'

Dr Oliver Joyce was a surgeon at the regional hospital in Galway. He had become friends with Mom and Dad years ago when he was scouting the area for an old farm cart to buy for the hospital auction. Dad had one and let him have it for free. Dr Joyce wanted to pay for it but Dad flatly refused, saying that money wouldn't buy our good health and may it always continue. Anyhow that started the friendship with Dr Joyce and he had kept in touch ever since. Mom and Dad each had a horse of their own and Dr Joyce was now used to riding either of them.

'That sounds great. We'll beat the heat and the flies and be back in time for a good breakfast,' Mom continued. 'We'll see you bright and early tomorrow. Take care now. Good-bye'

'Oliver? He's coming out to ride?' Dad asked, looking hassled. 'You know I can't cope with another thing.'

'Don't fret. I'll ride with him. He'll be here at

seven tomorrow morning. We'll be back before it gets too hot. Maybe Clare might take out Piggy. It's been a week since he had the antibiotic. We're only going for a walk down to the forestry. It might do him a world of good. What do you think?'

'I think you're right,' said Dad. He shouted in to me, 'Hey, how would you like to ride Piggy again?'

I pretended not to hear him. 'Dad, did you say something to me?'

'What a beautiful morning for a ride!' Dr Joyce exclaimed. 'You don't know how lucky you are to have this farm.' Little did he know, I thought to myself as I mounted Piggy.

Dr Joyce was a tall, light-framed man. By the way his hair had thinned and was grey around the edges, I guessed he was older than Dad. Dad's hair was still dark and bushy, with only a few gray ribs through it. Dr Joyce had piercing dark eyes, a cheerful smile, and the longest fingers that I ever had seen. When I described them to Maggie on one occasion she told me I was dense and should know that hospitals look at doctors' hands before they hire them to operate.

'Maggie,' I'd told her, 'what you don't know, you make up.'

Mom and I were dressed casually in flannel shirts, jeans, wellingtons, and riding-hats. Dr Joyce, on the other hand, was dressed in style. White breeches and leather boots, blue-checked shirt with scarf tucked in at the neck, light tweed jacket and a riding-hat – he looked ready for the Dublin Horse Show.

I could tell that Piggy was delighted to be ridden again. There was a spring in his step as we set off down the farmyard road to the nearby forestry. Mom led the way on her dapple-grey mare, River Run. Dr Joyce came next on Dad's big chestnut, Casey, and I brought up the rear on Piggy, with Rex and Tiny close behind. While Mom and the doctor chatted back and forth I let my mind wander, happy to be back on Piggy again.

It was cool; the dew had not yet cleared from the fields, where cattle and sheep were grazing or lying in the damp grass, but the bright sun heralded the start of another hot dry cloudless day. The air was fragrant with the smell of ripening berries that grew along the hedgerows and birds sang in the tall beech and chestnut-trees. Rex and Tiny darted about like young hares, criss-crossing the fields and roadways, picking up a scent, losing it and finding another.

Finally we reached the heavy timber gates that marked the entrance to the forestry. The gates were padlocked but a small bridle path at one side gave access to people and their dogs and horses. The trees shielded the sunlight and it was dark and moist along the path. Our voices echoed strangely and the noise of the dogs scampering in the undergrowth had an eerie sound. We walked on down the needle-strewn foresters' track, deeper into the heart of the woodland. We were in a mystical land of legend.

'How about a trot?' suggested Dr Joyce. The cool air and spongy footing had made the horses come alive.

'Why not? It'll get rid of the cobwebs,' Mom replied, urging River Run into a trot. Dr Joyce and I followed. Piggy took three strides. Then he began to cough. He tried to keep trotting with the other horses but couldn't. He was choking with the intensity of each hacking cough. He had to slow up and let the other horses move away from him.

Mom looked back on hearing him cough, and when she saw that we had stopped she called to Dr Joyce. They turned their horses and walked back to us. Piggy continued to cough, trying to clear his throat, and I could feel the tears trickle down my face.

'It's okay, Clare. We'll give him a chance to catch his breath and then we'll all walk home together,' Mom said.

I sat there on Piggy feeling helpless. Mom had said it was okay but I was worried. Was Piggy ever going to get better? And what about the Championship in Ballinasloe, one week from today?

'What's wrong with him?' asked Dr Joyce.

'He's had this cough for some weeks. John Moran, our vet, put him on a course of antibiotics and we were hoping it would have cleared by now. I suppose we were expecting too much,' Mom explained. 'Clare, he's better now. We'll head back. Now don't worry. We'll give John a ring when we get home.'

I was too crushed to say anything. I walked Piggy home on a loose rein, letting him stop to cough when he needed to. I heard Mom explaining to Dr Joyce about the Working Hunter Championship next Saturday, and about Nick and how hard we'd trained all summer for it.

I thought about it too: the competition, the judging, the rosettes, the victory gallop – it was all fading slowly away from me. But none of it would have mattered if only Piggy were well again.

We were just approaching the barley fields before the river when something Dr Joyce said caught my ear.

'My brother's wife used to have an old horse for riding. In the summertime, as I remember, he suffered from a terrible cough. It was only after several years of trying every remedy and household cure known that they stumbled on a combination of things that worked.'

I was all ears.

'What was it, Ollie?' asked Mom as we went over the bridge towards home.

'First of all, they changed the horse's bedding from straw to paper – they were able to buy big bales of cut-up newsprint from a large feed and hardware supplier.'

'Okay. What else?'

'I think she told me that they cut hay out of his diet completely – they switched him to a type of baled silage, also bought at the feed store.'

We had arrived at the yard. Mom, still mounted, was listening intently to Dr Joyce. 'And then there was one other thing they did. They got hold of this expensive powder that they added to the horse's feed.'

'Do you remember what it was called?'

I silently crossed my fingers for luck to help to jog his memory.

'Gosh, I'm not too sure. I suppose I could phone my sister-in-law and see if she remembers the name.'

'Oh, Ollie, please do.'

That night when I was in bed Mom came in. She didn't ask me why I was still awake.

It had been a long day. Frustrating hours of waiting for John to come and check out Piggy. Then hearing the verdict: Piggy's symptoms were still the same. The antibiotics hadn't worked.

'Dr Joyce just called,' said Mom, sitting on the edge of my bed. 'He gave me the name of the medicine that helped his sister-in-law's horse.'

I said nothing but tears welled up in my eyes. I seemed to have been on the verge of tears all day.

'Clare, it breaks my heart to see Piggy coughing and you upset. You've done so well with him this summer. We're proud of you... Now, I'm going to make a promise to you – I'll get Piggy better.... Now off to sleep.'

15 Mom Takes Charge

'Do you have it?' I heard Mom ask as I sat at the kitchen table, toying with a bowl of cereal. Sam was taking advantage of her absence to stick his whole arm down into the king-size box of cornflakes to look for the free toy enclosed. For once I didn't bother to complain.

'Great, I'm on my way. Will you wait for me? I'll be there in ten minutes. See you, John, and thanks.' I heard her laugh, then hang up the phone.

'John has the medicine,' she said when she came back into the kitchen. 'But we must hurry. I want to talk to him before he leaves on his calls. Sam, run out and tell Dad we're going to town and should be back in an hour.'

Then Mom pulled up a kitchen chair next to the dresser. We watched as she stood up on it, extracted something from an old tea-tin on the top, and put it into her pocket.

'What's that?' asked Sam.

'Never you mind,' said Mom, grabbing the jeep keys from the key rack and heading out towards the yard. 'Now, off you go to Dad.'

John Moran lived on the outskirts of the closest town to our village, in an old stone house with a high wall all around it. His animal clinic was set up in the stable yard across from the house. He was in his office waiting for us when we pulled in.

Nick appeared from around the side of the house. 'Any news?'

'Still the same. But Mom is getting him a new medicine.'

We all went into John's surgery. 'Clare,' said Mom, 'I want to talk to John for a minute. You go with Nick and say Hello to Mrs Moran.'

She gave me a look, meaning to scram.

'No, Mom,' I answered stubbornly. 'I want to hear what John says. Piggy is my pony and I'm staying.' I gave her a look back, meaning I wasn't budging. She started to argue but then changed her mind. Behind her back, Nick gave me a thumbs-up sign.

'What do you honestly think, John?' Mom asked.

'You know me. I'm a great believer in letting time and nature cure most ills. If he were mine I'd probably turn him out in a bare field for a month or two. But then there's this Championship.' He smiled at me.

'Here we are!' He took up a white plastic jar and examined the label. 'One level scoop of granules should be added to the pony's feed twice a day, for at least five days. It should…'

'Five days!' Mom interrupted excitedly. 'We can do it. Today is Monday, so we've got today, Tuesday, Wednesday, Thursday and Friday. That's five full days. We'll just have time.'

John shook his head, more in wonder than doubt. 'This treatment costs fifty quid – and there are no guarantees. It might not help Piggy in the slightest.'

'John, I know you think I'm daft and I probably am. But that's beside the point. I promised Clare last night that I would do whatever I could to help Piggy recover in time for the Championship.' She reached into her pocket and extracted several notes. 'Here's the fifty... Now, we'd better go back and start the treatment.'

'You go with them, Nick, if you like,' said John. 'I'll deal with Malone's sheep-dog on my own.'

As we walked out to the jeep, the secret of the tea-tin at the top of the dresser suddenly dawned on me. It was Mom's 'emergency' money and she was giving a chunk of it to me.

I felt all trembly inside as I squeezed her hand.

'Finished,' said Mom with a relieved sigh as she kicked out the last of the baled paper bedding around Piggy's stable. She and Nick and I had spent the last two hours removing ever speck of dirt and wisp of straw from it. We even disinfected the floor with Jeyes fluid. My tee-shirt was sticking to me and my hands and bare legs were black with dust and dirt. Nick didn't look much better.

'Can't we take a break?' I begged, dying for a long cool drink and a chance to sit down.

'Almost. Bring in Piggy and we'll feed him. The sooner we get the first dose into him the better. I'll get the feed ready.' She turned and said to Nick, 'We'd better do the silage as well. Get the knife from the bench in the tool-shed and open the bale Dad left in the yard. Then we'll all have a nice long rest.'

Nick went off, with Rex and Tiny at his heels. Tiny
knew from the bucket he carried that he was off to
the shed. He was a dinger for catching mice around
the stored sacks of grain and pony-nuts.

We were all too tired to talk much during dinner.
Dad was equally silent. When we had come in he'd
been sitting in the big armchair with his boots
propped up on a footstool watching TV. Strangely
Mom didn't say anything to him. She usually did
when she saw him inside on a fine day for work.

Afterwards it struck me as odd that, apart from
getting the bale of silage, he hadn't helped us at all.
Usually he was the one to direct anything involving
the livestock. I was glad we had had Nick with us.

When I saw Nick to the door he said, 'I'll come
over on Wednesday. If the powder works – and,' as
he saw my face droop, 'it *will* work – he should be
able to do a little light work then. Give him the rest
of the day and tomorrow to respond.'

When we fed Piggy his first dose of powder, Mom
had said to me, 'Now all we need is a small miracle.'

Well, it hadn't happened on Monday. Nor on
Tuesday – so far. True, he hadn't coughed when I
was in his stable in the afternoon. But that could
have been just coincidence. When I got back to the
house Maggie was there, to ask me round for tea.
But I was too depressed to go.

I went into the kitchen. Dad was sitting at the
table, half-heartedly looking at a paper. He looked

up and gave a weak 'Hi!' I didn't bother replying. All of a sudden I wanted somebody to talk to. Where was Mom? Even Sam would have been acceptable but he'd gone camping. Dad was useless at the moment. I was sorry I'd sent Maggie away.

I sat down in the armchair and began to cry very softly and silently. The Championship was only three days away and even if Piggy miraculously got better he'd have missed out a vital week's preparation. It was the end of a dream, a dream that had kept me going through all the hard work and effort. I thought I'd ring Nick later and tell him not to bother coming over next morning.

It must have been about an hour later when Mom walked in. She was dressed in a cotton skirt and shirt. I vaguely registered the fact – where had she been? Skirts were for formal occasions.

She sank into the chair and looked at us

'Oh, Mom,' I blurted out, 'Piggy isn't getting any better. I knew this was going to happen. He won't be ready for the Championship. Even if he gets better he won't have had any practice for over two weeks. We can't win now.'

'Clare!' Mom's voice had a new sharp tone. 'Pull yourself together.' She looked at Dad and said in an equally hard voice. 'Tom, what are you doing in the house at this time of day?'

He looked at her in surprise. So did I. Mom hardly ever spoke to anyone like that. Least of all us.

'I just didn't feel like work... it's wearing... all this uncertainty.'

'Well, there's no more uncertainty. I went to see Lynch. He's not going to sell the land. And he's adamant that the cows can't cross over it.... You were right about him, Clare. He's a rough, tough diamond.'

'What's going to happen now?' I piped in. Up to ten minutes ago my only worry was about the Championship. Now my whole world was crashing around me.

Dad looked equally stunned. 'You did what? ...That's the end of it then,' he muttered.

'No it's not. Now sit up, the pair of you, and listen to me. I've never come across such spineless dead-beats in my life. When the going gets tough you've got to fight.'

'But how can we? Take him to law, I suppose.'

'Clare, if you start to cry I'll send you away.... Now, Tom, think hard. Was your father a complete dunce?'

He looked bewildered. 'No, of course not.'

'Well that's something, though the way you've been carrying on for the last while I was beginning to think he might have been a half-wit.... He bought the grazing fields, didn't he?'

'Yes.'

'Would he have been fool enough to buy land with no way of getting to it?'

'But Paddy Gallagher promised him he could use the duck-pond meadow. He gave him a right of way.'

'And your father didn't copper-fasten it. Even though he knew Paddy Gallagher was an old man. That he had no family. That that piece of land would pass on to someone else.... No, I don't believe it. He must have got Paddy Gallagher to sign something giving the right of way. All we need is a written declaration, witnessed by someone – I checked that with O'Neill.'

'So what do we do?'

'First, find out when your father bought the grazing fields. Then take the house apart. There has to be a document somewhere – look for it.'

'Where?' Dad still looked shell-shocked. If it hadn't been so serious it would have been almost funny.

'Everywhere. Old boxes. Drawers. Cupboards. Old records. Ledgers. Files. Presses.' Seeing that Dad was about to say something else, she held up her hand. 'And if you can't find anything here, go down and take O'Neill's office apart.'

'Well, I suppose we'd better start.' Dad got to his feet.

'No, not "we". You. I've too much on my hands. Who do you think has been doing everything for Piggy all this time? Working like a beaver changing his bedding. Feeding him. Dosing him. Checking him on the hour, every hour.'

'I'm sorry, Mom,' I began, but she cut across me.

'I've done my bit. Now I'm off to take a bath. Get the tea, Clare. Something nice. I'm as hungry,' she smiled, 'as Maggie.' She disappeared upstairs.

'Come on, Clare,' said Dad with something like a return of his old spirit. 'We'll show her – that the Foxes aren't all half-wits.'

16 Two Miracles

'When will you try riding him again?' Nick asked.

It was Wednesday, and Nick, Maggie and I were scouting the hay-field for wild mushrooms. There hadn't been many on account of the dry weather, but I was hoping to surprise Dad with a basin full. He loved them baked, with a curl of butter in each.

'Mom said I could ride him tonight, just before dark, when the ground is dampish and the dust is down,' I replied. 'I'm very nervous. Do you think he could be better by now? We've only three days left before Ballinasloe.'

'Clare, you've got to stop worrying. What will be will be. We'll go to the show anyway and watch, if Piggy isn't up to it.'

'I'll be over tonight to cheer ye on,' Maggie said lightly, her high spirits never wavering. 'I'll bring Rambo for the crack.'

Maggie and I walked Rambo and Piggy around the front field. The sun, a bright orange ball, hung suspended above the tree-line in the western sky. The air was cool and damp as we rode around the edge of the field.

Piggy seemed perfect. No coughing. No snorting. He just seemed pleased to be at work again. But my heart was racing. What would happen when Mom asked us to trot? She stood in the middle of the field with Rex and Tiny at her feet, watching.

'Ride in for a minute,' she called, 'I want to talk to you.' We turned our ponies and walked towards her.

'Clare, I want you to lead. When you're ready, ask Piggy for a slow trot. Don't let him lunge forward or quicken. Keep it a slow, steady trot. Maggie, keep your distance whatever happens. Okay?'

'Right, Mom, but what will I do if he starts to cough?' I asked, with my head and heart pounding.

'Bring him back to a walk and let your reins loose, We'll take it from there. All set, girls?'

'Righto!' answered Maggie as she lined up Rambo behind Piggy and me.

'Here we go, boy,' I whispered to Piggy and urged him forward into a walk. I let him walk about a third of the field, then I nudged him with my heels to pick up a trot. He did so willingly. There was a suspended moment when it was as if nothing happened. It was like being balanced on a see-saw waiting for the other person to shift their weight. Piggy's health was the other person and the shift was between better and worse.

Then it came like a bad dream. He began to cough. He coughed three or four times and then snorted, was all right for a couple of strides, and then began coughing again. This time the cough was low and deep and persistent. I didn't have to slow him back to a walk. He did it himself.

I pulled him up and let him drop his head and cough.

'We'll try again tomorrow,' said Mom undeterred.

I turned away. As soon as I let the reins go I knew that Piggy still wasn't better.

'Come on, Clare. Look at the time,' Mom called from the yard. I looked down at my watch in the fading light. It was almost eight-thirty and soon it would be too dark to ride. I tightened Piggy's girth and led him out.

'Mom, it's not worth it. Let's phone the secretary and withdraw,' I said hopelessly. 'It's Thursday. There's only one day left.'

'Clare, you and your father are sounding more and more alike.' Mom sounded exasperated. 'Now go and walk Piggy around the front field for a few minutes until I join you.'

'Sorry, Mom.' I mounted Piggy and headed off towards the front field.

'When you're ready, pick up a slow trot. Nice and steady. Easy does it.' Her soothing voice drifted on the damp air around us, her sing-song tone almost hypnotising in the twilight. I pushed Piggy forward into a trot and waited for the inevitable.

The silence grew longer and longer. I didn't dare believe what was happening. Or, should I say, not happening. I was afraid to speak or even stir in the saddle.

We kept trotting a full circle and a half before the cough finally came. I slowed Piggy back to a walk and let him cough freely. He coughed two or three times, then snorted and snorted again. We continued to walk in the darkness.

'Try it again, Clare,' Mom's voice called softly across the field. I could barely make out where we were going but I obeyed. Piggy readily picked up a trot and once again we trotted around the edge of the field. He snorted but this time did not cough.

'Clare, extend your trot,' I heard her call. I was never allowed to even walk a pony when it was this dark. And here was Mom telling me to trot faster. I urged Piggy forward, hoping he could see where he was going. We trotted three full circuits before Mom's voice reached us again.

'That's enough, Clare. Bring him in.'

When I walked back to Mom she said nothing but led us by the bridle back to the yard. We untacked Piggy and made sure he had water and a fist of silage for the night. Mom switched off the light and as we walked towards the house she took my hand. I knew that something good was beginning to happen.

'It's a bloody miracle,' exclaimed Nick the next morning. 'I can't believe it. Pinch me to make sure I'm not dreaming.' He was standing in the middle of the hay-field, watching me canter Piggy slowly around the edge of the field. He cantered in a rhythmic rocking-horse manner as if he had been in training all along.

'I don't know what to say except that it's mighty and I'm so happy for you, Clare.' Nick sounded over the moon. 'We'll have to jump him over a couple of fences this evening to make sure he's fit enough to compete tomorrow. Wait until I tell Uncle John.'

That evening Mom, John Moran, Nick and Maggie stood outside the sand-ring watching me jump. Nick had set up four fences similar in height and width to the ones that would be at Ballinasloe and had carefully watered the ground to eliminate as much dust as possible.

'Okay, Clare, when you're ready,' he instructed. 'Remember to keep your canter even and Piggy pulled together. Just like we were working on before he got sick. Off you go.'

After once around the course, Nick called us in. 'Great stuff! That's enough for tonight. We'll give him a few jumps in the morning before we go. What

do you think, Uncle John?'

'I think I'd better listen to this farmer's wife more often,' said John with a grin. 'I never thought the powder would work in such a short space of time. It just shows that the pony's wind passages and lungs were very irritated.... Where's the boss, by the way? Why isn't he here for the revelation?'

'Probably in the house, John. It's been a tough few weeks with...' Mom's explanation was suddenly interrupted by a loud Indian war-call.

'What in God's name is that?' exclaimed Nick.

The whooping came closer and next thing Dad appeared at the stable door, piggybacking Sam who was home from his camping trip. He was punching the air.

We all looked dumbfounded.

'All you all right?' asked Mom.

'Couldn't be any better!' Dad continued to dance around. Then he came to a halt, put Sam down and turned to Mom.

'Remember the night you said my dad couldn't have been so stupid that he'd buy the grazing fields without making sure he had a permanent right of way across the duck-pond meadow?'

'Yes, but what...'

'You said that only for looking after Piggy you'd have taken the house apart to see if you could find anything.'

'And?'

'I've spent the last three days going through everything and guess what I found?'

He waved a piece of paper at us.

'Where did you find it?...For God's sake be careful. It'll blow away.'

Back in the kitchen, we all, in turn, examined the yellowed paper. It was short and to the point:

5th of September 1939

I, Paddy Gallagher of Clarinbeg, the owner of the well field beside the river Clarin, adjoining the Fox farm, hereby permit James Fox, also of Clarinbeg, and kin and descendants to drive his animals from his land at Clarinbeg across this field to the grazing fields he bought from me.

Signed: Paddy Gallagher   *Witness:* Father Joe Keane
Parish Priest, Clarinbeg.

'So we have a right of way for all time. I'll tell O'Neill to get on to it straight away. And he can tell old Lynch to go to hell.' Dad was jubilant.

'He'll probably sell to you now,' said Mom.

'We don't need to buy it.'

I couldn't believe the change of mood that had come over Dad. He was glowing with happiness.

'Buy it,' said Mom, 'and be done with it.'

'I'd listen to her, Tom,' said John, winking at me. 'She knows what's what.'

That night I crept downstairs to check my jodhpur boots were polished. Everyone had gone, except

Mom and Dad who were in the kitchen talking.

'I still don't understand why you suddenly hit on the idea that there had to be a document,' said Dad.

'It was the locked gate. Remember, you said that when your father bought the grazing fields he put in a gate from the farm so that the cows could get into the duck-pond meadow. I figured he wouldn't have gone to all that expense unless he was pretty sure he had a *permanent* right of way through the meadow.'

'Why didn't I think of that?' chuckled Dad.

'Because you're a busy working man. I'm only a housewife. Nothing to do all day except sit around and think!... One thing puzzles me though. If old Paddy Gallagher gave that letter to your father, surely he, or his solicitor, would have a copy. And it should have been with the deeds of the Gallagher land that your father bought.'

'Maybe. Maybe not. Maybe Paddy Gallagher never gave it to his solicitor – if he had one. Maybe the nephew came across it and realised it would take from the value of the land Lynch was buying.'

'Or maybe it was with the deeds and Lynch found it and decided to say nothing about it. Trusting that you might have lost the original.'

'Surely he wouldn't.'

'You never know... By the way, where *did* you find it?'

'Stuck into an old farm ledger, as a page mark.'

I crept upstairs again. I was sorry for Kelly. If Mom's suspicion was true, it must be pretty awful having a father like that.

17 Ballinasloe

Dawn broke early and the whole family was up with it. There was so much to do to get ready for the show. What with all the excitement about Dad's find, the decision to take Piggy wasn't made until after supper last night. And a late supper at that. John, Nick and Mom agreed that, regardless of fitness and training, I should compete. John added that while it was important not to push Piggy I should ride for the fun of it and the experience.

I was still pinching myself and trying to believe that Piggy was really well again, when Mom's harassed voice reached me. 'Clare, will you stop your day-dreaming and do something. We still need to get the jeep packed and the five-gallon can filled with water.... Oh, don't bother – I'll do it myself. You'd better get dressed and leave the rest to me.'

'Mom, will the jumps be really high?' I asked. 'You know I'm not able to jump a full barrel. I hope Nick gets here soon. He'll help me to school Piggy over a spread.'

'Clare, there's no time for anything except to get loaded and be on our way. The Championship starts at ten o'clock. Remember, we decided last night that we wouldn't school Piggy this morning.'

'But, Mom, I've just got to practise.' I could feel my nerve beginning to go.

'Clare, get a move on,' ordered Mom. 'You've ten minutes to be dressed and sitting in the jeep? Understand?'

I turned and headed up the back stairs to change. As I did, I heard Nick's confident voice like a breath of fresh air.

'Hi, sorry we're late. What can we do?'

Now everything would be all right. Mom would leave Nick in charge of me. That suited me down to the ground. Probably as a reaction from all the tension of Piggy, Mom and I had been getting on each other's nerves lately.

We arrived at the Ballinasloe showgrounds at exactly nine, a regular entourage with Morans, O'Connors and Foxes in a car, lorry and jeep.

The parking lot for the competitors at the show was already jammed with every kind of horse-box and lorry. Sam couldn't wait to get a closer look at them.

The weather had changed with the month. A cool September breeze blew under a ceiling of dark thunder clouds. Despite my wool jacket, a shiver ran through me when I got out of the jeep. I felt cold and nervous. My heart started to race when my eye caught sight of the arena set up with fences.

I clutched Maggie. 'Mags, I feel sick. Piggy's not able for this. It's not fair to him. Will you tell Mom for me?'

'Clare, will ye stop spoutin'?' Maggie rolled her eyes. 'It's only a show. I've got meself a fiver. Let's see if there's a sweet shop about.'

'You go. I'd better stay with Piggy,' I said, sinking down on top of the picnic basket.

'Clare, tell Dad and Sam I've gone to get your number and see how soon the Championship will start. I've told Nick to find your ring and see when we can walk the course. Why don't you give Piggy a rub with a soft cloth?' Mom said as she hurried off in the direction of the offices.

I was about to say something but she disappeared behind the line of parked vehicles before I could open my mouth.

'Great!' I mumbled to myself as I by-passed the cloth, took the hoof-pick out of the grooming kit and mindlessly stabbed at the grass beneath my feet. No Dad. No Nick. No Mom. Where was everyone when I needed them?

'Hi, Clare!' A faintly familiar voice startled me. 'How's Piggy?'

I looked up and, to my amazement, saw Kelly Lynch standing in front of me, dressed in her riding-clothes and looking her usual elegant self.

I gulped a few times before I managed to say, 'He's okay.'

We stood in silence for a few moments, neither of us knowing what to say next. Then Kelly spoke.

'You forgot your hair-slide. Vera found it rolled up in the picnic rug last week-end when she was unpacking the boot.' She held out my cheap plastic hair-clip – Vera would have known it couldn't belong to Kelly.

I stood up and took it from her, wanting to hide the ugly thing as soon as I could.

'Thanks. You needn't have bothered, it's only an old one,' I said stuffing it into my pocket.

'Are you riding in the Championship?'

'I suppose so but I'm not sure. Piggy is only just better and he's not really fit.' I was still hoping that, somehow or other, I wouldn't have to ride. 'Mom just wants me to do it for the fun of it.'

'You're lucky... I wish I could do it just for fun.' Kelly looked down at the ground. 'Dad expects me to win the class. He's asked some of his business friends here to watch me and then they'll come back to the house for a barbecue to celebrate.'

'You'll do fine, Kelly. You're a super rider and you've got a smashing pony,' I said. I couldn't really believe I was saying this to her. But I meant it. I felt sorry for anyone with a dad like hers.

'I'd better go,' said Kelly.

'See you... and thanks for my clip,' I called after her.

'Consorting with the enemy?' Nick said smiling as he strode up and leaned against the horse-box next to me. 'What was that all about?'

'Nothing,' I mumbled as I went back to stabbing the grass.

'Come on. We'll walk the course before you warm up. We don't have much time,' said Nick, dragging me to my feet. 'I think you're in for a surprise.'

'So what,' I asked listlessly. 'I feel rotten and nobody cares.'

Nick took me firmly by the arm and half pulled me across the car park.

'You're not going to believe this,' he chuckled as we entered the show-ring.

'Nick!' I stared in awe at the first fence. 'It's just like the one we practised over at home.'

I measured the top rail of the fence against the second button of my riding-jacket (a built-in measuring device I often used with Maggie during our practice sessions at home; Maggie always insisted that I wear my jacket – she maintained it was the done thing at all the big showyards).

'Nick, it's the same height, the same width, the same everything. How could I be so lucky?' I still couldn't believe it.

'And the rest are the same. Good honest fences. No spooky cottages. Now we'd better get going. It's getting late and we have to walk the course before you warm up.'

I turned and followed him, thinking to myself, 'I can do it. I know I can,' imitating Dad by punching the air with a clenched fist inside my open jacket.

A light rain had begun to fall as we walked around the course, discussing each fence's approach and the best places to check and change leads. There were nine in all, including a double. One had water underneath it, but I wasn't worried. Piggy and I often cantered through pools of water.

Nick felt fence three – an old shed door set upright on its side – was the one to be careful of. It looked a lot higher and more difficult from a distance. And because the approach meant going away from the entrance gate, it could pose a problem for a pony intent on going home.

Mom was in the horse-box when we went back to the jeep. She had Piggy tacked up with a light waterproof over his saddle.

'Good, you're back,' she called from the opened jockey door of the trailer. 'I've got your number,' handing me a tie-on strip with the number 303 printed on it. 'And you're jumping third.'

Nick lowered the ramp and let Piggy out. 'Better get him warmed up.'

'Clare, pull out your rain jacket.' Mom looked up towards the dark, cloud-covered sky. 'Put on this one, Nick. Maggie, do you need one?'

'Thanks,' said Maggie struggling to get her arms into the waxed jacket. 'Ye look like a champ, Clare. I saw them lads from the *Tribune* takin' photos. Maybe they'll take one of ye and Piggy? Will I ask them?'

'Mags! That's the last thing I need right now.'

I mounted Piggy and settled my feet into the stirrups. The shower of rain had passed, leaving a clean, fresh scent in the air. I took a deep breath as we made our way to the warm-up ring.

'One more jump should do it,' Nick instructed from the centre of the ring. It was jammed with competitors trying to get ready for the Championship class. It was all I could do to keep from bumping into another pony. Piggy's ears lay flat back, showing his annoyance at being jostled and crammed inside the small enclosure. I saw Kelly having trouble with Moonstepper.

'That's plenty for Piggy,' said Nick. 'Walk him around outside to keep him warm and settled.'

The air was crisp but I didn't feel the cold. My insides were now on fire with a raging battle of emotions – fear, reluctance, courage, determination.

As we went towards the show-ring I saw the judge. He was a heavy-set middle-aged man, wearing a tan mackintosh and a black bowler hat. He was chatting with the ring steward and assistant. I liked his round jolly face and low booming laugh.

First in the ring was a boy from County Kildare riding a fine-boned chestnut pony. The pony was eager to get away from the rider's tight rein and lunged forward every time the boy let him off, three strides from the fence. After each, he was quickly brought back, so the result was not flowing and even paced. Clear round, however.

The second pony, from County Antrim, dug his feet into the base of the first fence and refused to jump it. Despite a smack from the whip, he refused a second time, then a third time. Eliminated! My heart did a flip-flop. Nick must have sensed my nervousness and was beside me in seconds.

'Clare, listen to me. There's nothing wrong with that fence. That girl had no control over her pony. You must ride on at each fence. Do you hear me?'

All I heard was the loudspeaker: 'The next rider is Clare Fox from County Galway. Riding Timber Twig.' It was always a shock to hear Piggy called by his real name!

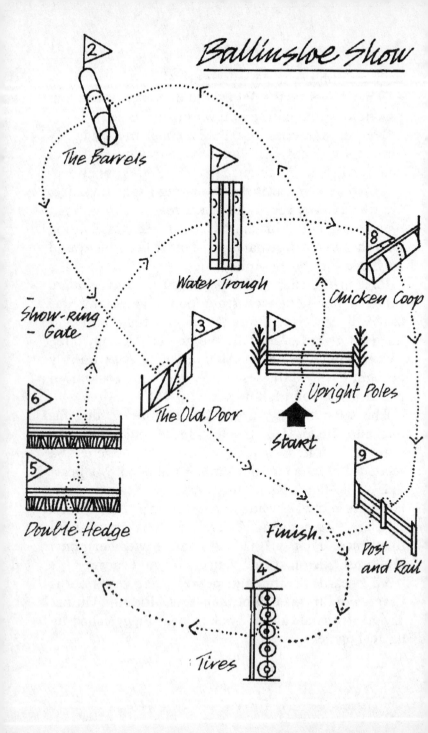

As I went into the ring my eyes fell on a solid wall of supporters – Mom, Dad, Sam, Maggie, John and Nick. The odious Brenda Fahy was also there.

After saluting the judge, I trotted Piggy to the bottom of the ring. He felt strong and eager as I headed for the first fence.

Remembering the last rider and Nick's advice to 'ride on', I nudged Piggy into a forward moving pace and he jumped it easily. We cantered on to the top of the ring and flew over the barrel fence. Now for the gate. I gave Piggy a slight slap on his shoulder but there was no difficulty; he soared over it. On to the tyre fence, a change of lead, up and over it. 'Easy, boy, easy,' I coaxed as we approached the double. 'Three – two – one – now!' he shot through it as if the two poles were sticks on the ground.

'Now, where?' I asked myself, then remembered – the water jump. After that it was the chicken coop and the final was the post-and-rail. He went over that like a steeplechaser. A roar went up from the railings and I knew I had had a great round.

Outside the ring, the family gathered around. Nick patted Piggy. 'You've a good chance of being called back.'

I didn't really care at this stage. I had done my best. Piggy was in top form. He hadn't coughed once. Nothing else mattered. I didn't watch the other competitors, though Maggie told me that Kelly had a clear round, even though Moonstepper was acting up at times. I loosened Piggy's girth and let Nick drape a cover over his rump to keep him warm.

The loudspeaker crackled and a silence descended on the crowd. 'Will the following numbers please return to the ring in the order called. Number 303...'

My number! Called first! I had been called back in first place. I couldn't believe it.

'Great,' said Nick, adding his voice to the other congratulations. 'Now hold him together.'

After trotting around the ring twice, we changed direction. Then we were called in towards the centre. I was at the head of the line, Kelly was in fourth place. I knew this next phase would be the hardest for Piggy and me. Though Piggy now looked remarkably trim, there were showier ponies in the line.

The ring steward called me forward. The judge looked at Piggy's conformation, asked me to walk forward on a straight line, trot back and canter on for my figure-of-eight.

I trotted to the top of the ring, planning ahead as Nick had instructed me. I took my bearings. Where to start, where to change direction. I was conscious that both circles must be even and the same size. Left lead canter. Right lead canter. Keep the pace even.

'Good boy,' I praised as I headed to the outer edge of the ring for the gallop. We flew like the wind down the long side. I checked him as we reached the other corner, steadied him back to a canter, then a trot, before returning to the judge. I halted and saluted before returning to my place in line.

I watched the other competitors. How well they were all schooled! I felt my chances were slim. But I knew I had done well and that was the main thing. Moonstepper was not behaving well. He pawed the ground nervously and shook his head, trying to snatch the reins from Kelly's hands as she stood in line.

'Overtraining and too much grain,' Nick had diagnosed after the Scariff incident. All to please Con Lynch. I felt sorry for Kelly – though at the back of my mind I had the feeling she was well able for him. She wanted to win as much as he did. Still maybe Maggie and I could ask her over to gather branches and rotten bales for the Hallowe'en bonfire. That is, if she hadn't disappeared off to some swank boarding-school.

The loudspeaker sprang into life. I was jolted back to reality. The result was about to be announced.

'The Working Hunter Champion for this year is Timber Twig, ridden by Clare Fox from County Galway.'

18 The Parting of the Ways

It all seemed like a dream when we finally got home from the show. The endless shaking of hands and posing for photographs coming on top of the nervous strain of the competition, not to mention the lack of sleep the night before, had left me exhausted. I didn't feel like talking to anyone. I just wanted to be alone. I leaned up against the wall in Piggy's stable and watched him happily munch on a forkful of silage. His sturdy neck and body rippled with new muscles, the result of our weeks of hard training. I thought to myself how much I loved him. And now he had given me the gift of an all-Ireland champ-ionship.

'Clare, Clare, where are ye?' I heard a familiar voice bellow. I latched Piggy's stable door, took a deep breath and headed out to see what my other best friend wanted.

'Here, Mags,' I answered. 'Just checking to see if Piggy had enough water.'

'Nick is looking for ye. He's got something in a bag to give ye. Quick! C'mon, he's waiting out the front.'

We tore across the yard like two young children racing to queue up for the ice-cream van. My energy had returned.

'Nick, she's here,' Maggie yelled as we turned the corner of the house and found him looking over the

136

timber-railed fence at the mares and foals. Tucked under his arm was a plastic bag.

'Did you want me, Nick?' I asked bashfully.

I could never think of things to say when I was embarrassed. Why couldn't I be a little more like Maggie, able to prattle on about almost everything and anything?

'What's in the bag?' asked Maggie, curiosity getting the better of her.

'It's for Clare,' said Nick, handing it to me. 'It's a kind of congratulations–best-of-luck present from Uncle John and me.'

'Open it.'

Shyly I took the bag from him and looked inside.

'What is it, Clare? Let me see.' Maggie grabbed the bag from me. I had already seen what lay neatly folded inside.

'Jodhpurs! Oh, Clare, ye lucky so and so,' Maggie babbled. 'They're just like Kelly's. Same colour and everything.' She now had them out of the bag and was holding them up to her waist.

'Thanks a million, Nick,' I mumbled. 'You and your uncle really shouldn't...'

'Why not? Think of what you've done for my reputation as a trainer! Maybe I'll be asked to coach the Irish Olympic team... Seriously, you and Piggy did great.'

'And now it's all over,' said Maggie. 'Back to the books next week.'

'When are you off, Nick,' I asked. It seemed strange to think I wouldn't be seeing him every day any more.

'Day after tomorrow.'

If only Mom were here. She'd have asked him over tomorrow night. But she wasn't. I braced myself.

'Can you come over tomorrow night for supper?'

'Can't. Got a prior engagement.'

I must have looked as deflated as I felt because he immediately smiled at me and said, 'I'll be over in the morning to say good-bye to your mom and dad. But I'll see *you* tomorrow evening.'

He laughed, got on his bike and cycled down the road.

'What did he mean?' I asked Maggie.

'Come on in. Yer mam has a message for ye.'

Mom had. Kelly had phoned to ask if I would go to dinner at The Lobster Pot, the Lynchs' seafood restaurant, tomorrow night. She'd asked Maggie as well. And Nick.

'Ain't she the witch?' said Maggie raising her eyebrows as we ate a toasted cheese sandwich. We were in the sitting-room before a cheerful fire, welcome after the chill of the outside air. Mom had drawn the curtains before she and Dad had gone out over the duck-pond meadow to check the cows. It was the beginning of autumn.

I was glad to be seeing Nick again but I wished it was in the old familiar setting of home. I wasn't sure about The Lobster Pot. I wished I looked as good as Kelly. And could talk as much as Maggie.

'I know what I'll have,' said Maggie. 'Jumbo prawns and that super chocolate cake. I wonder who'll be there – apart from us three. Maybe the gorilla will show. And Mrs Gorilla, clanking with gold bracelets.'

'I wonder will Brenda Fahy be there,' I said.

She wasn't.
But that's another story.

Glossary

Walk: A four-beat gait. The pony puts each foot down individually.

Trot: A two-beat gait. The pony uses its legs in diagonal pairs.

Canter: A three-beat gait. The pony starts by putting down one hind leg. Then he puts down the other hind leg with the opposite front leg. He then puts down the other front leg, which is called the leading leg.

Gallop: A four-beat gait. The pony starts by putting down one hind leg. He then puts down the other hind leg. Next he puts down the opposite front leg, followed by the other front leg.

Canter lead: A term used to describe the pony's leading leg. When the pony is cantering to the left, the left front leg should be leading; when cantering to the right, the right front leg should be leading.

Wrong lead: When the pony is cantering to the left with the right front leg leading, or cantering to the right with the left front leg leading.

Figure-of-eight: A pattern used as a riding exercise. It is made up of two connected circles ranging from 10 to 20 meters wide. The rider must make his or her pony bend around each circle, changing direction where the two circles join. Both circles must be equal in size.

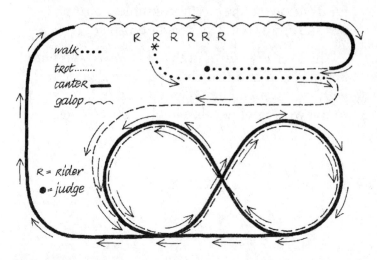

Lead-rein class: A showing class for ponies not exceeding 123 cms measured at the wither, the point where the pony's back and neck meet. The pony has to be ridden by a child under the age of eight years. The pony and rider walk and trot. They must be led by a person over the age of sixteen years.

Working hunter pony class 133: A class for ponies not exceeding 133 cms and ridden by a child who is under the age of fourteen on the 1st of January. The class is judged on both jumping performance and a combination of manners, conformation, and movement. The pony and rider must do an individual test that often includes a figure-of-eight.

KATE McMAHON was born and educated in Massachusetts. She moved to County Galway, Ireland, in 1980, and set up a teaching service for dyslexic children. She continues to tutor privately and train teachers in this field.

She lives on a farm in the west of Ireland with her husband and two children. Her experiences with children and her keen interest in horses led to the writing of her first book, *Timber Twig*.

THE CHILDREN'S PRESS

Pauline Devine
Best Friends
A story about Sarah and her pony Bluebell. About triumphs and near-tragedies. About the shifting world of young friendships where loyalties ebb and flow.
192 pages. Illustrated. £3.95 paperback.

Pauline Devine
Riders by the Grey Lake
Eithne has problems, and cousin Mandy thinks she's 'weird'. Then one day a strange boy on a magnificent white horse comes towards her from the lake – and she finds herself torn between two worlds.
144 pages. Illustrated. £3.95 paperback.

Mary Arrigan
Dead Monks and Shady Deals
Holidaying in 'boring, snoring' Kildioma, Maeve feels brain deadness coming on. Then she meets 'drop-dead gorgeous' Fergus. Meanwhile sinister events are unfolding at the nearby abbey.
144 pages. Illustrated. £3.95 paperback.

Mary Arrigan
Landscape with Cracked Sheep
Nothing *ever* happens in Glengowan. But suddenly, this summer, Maeve, Leo and Jamie, in search of a lost family heirloom, find themselves involved in excitement and drama galore.
128 pages. Illustrated. £3.96 paperback.

THE CHILDREN'S PRESS

Yvonne MacGrory
The Ghost of Susannah Parry

Who was Susannah Parry? Does she haunt her deserted home? One dark October evening Brians spends two hours there. When he comes out he has changed utterly.
128 pages. Illustrated. £3.95 paperback.

Mary Arrigan
Seascape with Barber's Harp

Invited to Baltimore where Jamie's family is spending summer, Maeve and Leo get involved in a mysterious affair involving two Spaniards. Spanish gold?
The third Maeve Morris adventure.
160 pages. Illustrated. £3.95 paperback.

Terry Myler
Drawing Made Very Easy

Terry Myler starts at the very beginning – how to hold a pencil, goes on to teach hand control, shading, how to draw simple objects and give them shape 'If you can write, you can draw,' she says.
32 pages. £2.95 paperback.

Sarah Webb
Kids Can Cook

Kids love cooking and here's a cook-book specially for them. Easy recipes – easy to read easy to follow – all tried and tested by a panel of under-10s. Including recipes from well-know children's authors.
112 pages. Illustrated. £3.95 paperback.